MW00745064

*Home is the Sailor
Under the Sea*

Home is the Sailor
Under the Sea

MERMAID STORIES

Stephen Spotte

CREATIVE ARTS BOOK COMPANY
Berkeley ✦ California 94710

Home is The Sailor, Under the Sea is published
6by Donald S. Ellis and
distributed by Creative Arts Book Company.

For information contact:
Creative Arts Book Company
833 Bancroft Way
Berkeley, California 94710
(800) 848-7789

The characters, places, incidents, and situations
in this book are imaginary and have no relation
to any person, place, or actual happening.

ISBN 088739-266-0
Library of Congress Catalog Number 99-61372

Printed in the United States of America

To son Mike
Connoisseur of mermaids

There's another fish, the *Goofang*, that swims backward to keep the water out of its eyes. It's described as "about the size of a sunfish, only much bigger."

Jorge Luis Borges,
The Book of Imaginary Beings

Contents

BLOWDOWN

LATE AT NIGHT I HEAR JAMBAL COUGHING. THE DEEP SOUND OF IT raises goose pimples. I can't help feeling cold, and here it is July. Not even a blanket can take away the chill.

Twenty years ago Jambal killed a man. Hearing him now makes me sad. For him. For me. Especially for Junior. I can't sleep during set-up, which doesn't help. A new town brings hope. Every third day, hope. I look outside where our roustabouts have rigged temporary lights making the rain puddles shimmer like gasoline.

I lie awake with stuff running through my head. Teenie used to get after me for thinking too much. Thoughts only make the hurting worse, she said. Better to be like Marvie the Geek, who only does what he is told, nothing more. Marvie comes when you call him, like a dog. Marvie will never know the awful truth, Teenie used to say, and for that he's better off than you or me.

I could write them down, my thoughts and hers. Most of us don't leave any record. We breathe the air, drink the water; we die. We're air-takers, no better than insects. I could write if I wanted to. I can slide a pen across paper well enough. My handicap doesn't interfere. Teenie schooled me on the road. Once I took a correspondence course on writing. The advice was to write about what you understand best, but I'm not so sure. I think people write about what confuses them most,

1

the things they can never tell to another person except maybe in a letter or a story.

I miss Teenie. Sometimes I wonder about my dad—who he was. Teenie never said. She told me it wasn't important. All I know is he works with the circus, or did. I've watched them grow old and die, one by one: Jocko in that blowdown in Kentucky, Wysep shot by an Alabama townie, the others . . . I used to study their faces, but finding a resemblance to somebody is hard. I don't look like anyone else who was ever born.

I used to dream Junior was my dad because he remembered birthdays. Not just mine, everybody's. Junior got careless cleaning up after the big cats, and Jambal killed him. I heard his screams. Late at night we were ready to move out. Circus people are close-mouthed. We take care of our own. We left on schedule, and it could have been any of us in that wet grave. I'll probably be in one myself someday.

We lost Junior alive, and we lost him dead too. I doubt if anyone could ever find where he's buried. Train tracks go first to one horizon and then the next, always looking the same, on and on before merging into one straight line that goes forever. We crossed a section of track in the night. Some men got out of the trucks with shovels and scrambled down into a swale. They took Junior with them. I remember looking out at loosestrife blooming tall and purple in the lights. I still have the little porcelain dog Junior gave me when I turned ten. One ear was chipped from the start. Like Teenie said, nobody arrives perfect in this life or leaves that way either.

The days look best through a trailer window, and even better with the curtains pulled. Then I see only light and shadow; heat and cold are memories, and so are faces. I like it when cloud shadows darken the land and the wind pushes them aside, brightening everything again. It lets you know there's change in the world, that nothing stays the same.

When Teenie was around she slept from tear-down in one town through set-up in the next. She was too fat to lie in a bed or even sit on the doniker in our tiny bathroom. She used a blue bucket for the last function and a red one for washing herself. I'd listen to her snoring in the chair, hear the interruptions when her apnea took over.

I kept her little doilies she laid on the chair arms when set-up was over, like we had arrived in our permanent home.

With Teenie gone I'm alone in the trailer. Louie drives the pickup that pulls it. It's Louie who fills my tank and makes sure the water is warm. I'm in the water an hour before the big show and another hour after blow-off when people come out of the Big Top and mill around on the Midway. I'm one of the freaks in the Sideshow. Louie also brings my meals from the pie car because I can't walk. If not Louie, another rousta-bout, but I'm glad to have him and not someone else. Louie never looks at you. I thought at first it was because of my face . . . you know, because I'm so ugly. But I've noticed he never looks at anyone; instead, he looks off to the side and squints as if the light is brighter over there. He doesn't say much. Nobody knows where Louie is from, and as to where he's headed, it's where we're all headed.

One time outside of Huntington I couldn't take it anymore and I crawled away in the night. Teenie and Louie found me shivering behind an old stump, wet and crying, and Louie carried me home. I'd like to do something normal just once. I'd like to just stand up—not even walk, but stand—on real feet, real legs. People think the circus life is glamorous. Sure, I've traveled all over the South, but it isn't the same as going on a date or eating an ice cream cone that didn't come from Concessions.

When we got back to the trailer Teenie said to think of all the bored girls working at the five and dime and how they'd give a leg just to be Myrna the Mermaid for a single day. I said, I'll take that leg and another besides. Give me two legs and that's exactly how many I'd have. Two legs instead of this *thing*, and I'd trade jobs with the first girl who walked in the door. By then we were all crying, and Louie was patting me on the head. I felt terrible and told them I was sorry.

Sometimes I'll be splashing around in my tank and a woman with little kids will come up and peer over the edge. I wonder what it's like being her, a wife and mother. Does she get bored always coming back to the same house, or would it be nice having a permanent place and neighbors? Maybe a dog or cat so lazy it doesn't wake up when you shove the vacuum around. A flower bed and a husband to say you look nice now and again. Then one of the kids will yell, wow, is she really that ugly? And the mom will reply, naw, it's just a costume, and we got to go or Dad will be pissed. I look at her closer and see she has a shiner underneath the makeup, and then I think how everybody has problems.

Well, once again I've thought myself to daylight. When I pull back the curtain beside my bed a rosy glow is making everything look prettier. Maybe if I pulled myself outside and lay down in it . . . maybe. The rain has stopped. Cigarette filters are bobbing in the puddles like tiny boats. There's mud everywhere. I see we've set up in a field somewhere. I believe we're in Mississippi, but don't really remember or care. What's the difference? Teenie used to keep me posted on our whereabouts, but Louie never talks. I could ask him, but what's the point?

Some roustabouts come around the corner drinking coffee and laughing. They point to something in a nearby tree, a hornet's nest. The nest is gigantic, intricate. It hangs suspended in the air like a fat gray balloon. I think it looks beautiful. The time it took to build that nest! But time means nothing to hornets; they have no sense of it. The nest is their home. All that work, and a roustabout douses it with gasoline and strikes a match. The roustabouts laugh, but only for a minute. A minute is all the time it takes for the nest to disappear. They drop their empty cups in the puddles and leave. Jambal roars from the backyard. He's hungry.

There's a knock and Louie comes in with a breakfast tray: fried eggs, bacon, buttered toast, grits, juice, coffee. I don't feel hungry and think I'll just have coffee. Eat, Louie tells me, and leaves. He knows I won't. When Teenie was here Louie brought four breakfasts. Teenie ate three and most of mine. Got to train, she'd say with a laugh. I'm the Fat Lady, ain't I?

She had the most delicate fingers and toes for someone so

big, not like on a fat person at all. I envied her those. She called me her skinny little fish.

Dust floats across shafts of sunlight, drifting, searching for a place to settle. I'm like the dust. Just once it might have happened, a long time ago. Set-up was outside Harlan, Kentucky. We'd come in from Virginia the previous night and crossed the Cumberland Plateau. I always knew where we were back then because Teenie looked it up in her atlas. Now I don't care. During my show I noticed a man staring at me, but I was used to it. Men stare at me for lots of reasons, and I try to ignore them.

That night, in our trailer, there was a knock. Come in! Teenie yelled, thinking it was a circus neighbor or maybe Louie, but it was this same man, I'm sure of it. I was in the bedroom, but heard everything. Look, the man said, I'm a doctor, a special kind of surgeon, and I can make her better: cut the webbing from between her fingers, remove the areas of skin on her face that resemble scales, and so on. In appearance, she'd look almost normal. There wouldn't be any cost because I'm a professor at the university. Teenie listened, not getting up out of her chair. Thanks, she said, but we ain't interested.

I cried when the door closed. Teenie came to where I was lying in the dark. I wanted so much to be like everyone else. Teenie said, There, there, honey, don't worry. We can't sink roots here, we got a contract. And anyway, think of your career. Then she left and a few minutes later I heard the snores. For a while I hated her, but she was my only family. The mean feelings didn't last.

Funny how everything happens at once, then months and years go by when every day is the same as every other day, and each night is like the one before. The next afternoon a tornado came through. Blowdown! The main tent came crashing to the ground when the center pole and quarter poles got knocked aside like bowling pins. Fortunately, the townies were outside on the Midway. No one got hurt except Jocko, a roustabout, and he was killed where he stood. That's probably the only time I've felt truly left out. There I was in my tank with everyone else running around helping. Even the cooks were pulling on canvas. I paddled for three hours before Louie remembered and yanked me out.

That night I couldn't get warm. Outside, the air was chilly, and a thick fog drifted down from the mountains. When I pushed the curtain aside, everything was gray. The circus had shut down for repairs, and after working hours Teenie and some others had gone into town. The lot was quiet as death except for the elephants shuffling and tossing hay on their backs, and Jambal grumbling. Then the door opened, and I heard someone walking around. No lights were on. A voice said, Myrna, it's me. The voice belonged to Wysep, Jocko's brother, a dishwasher in the pie wagon.

I didn't answer. Wysep was drunk. I could smell the whiskey on him. He stumbled into the bedroom and sat down on the bed and started to cry. I reached out and touched his shoulder, and he sort of tumbled over on top of me. He held me for the longest time before falling asleep. He slept beside me all that night, the happiest night of my life. I felt his warmth in the darkness, the closeness of someone; I remember us touching. Before light, when he woke up, he turned scared and apologetic, but I told him, come back anytime. I never mentioned the incident to Teenie. Wysep didn't come again, and two weeks later, in Alabama, a townie shot him. Because he was black, Teenie said. That's all I know. I felt terrible then and still do.

People don't really want variety in their lives, they want sameness, and they know their luck is holding if nothing ever happens. Like this old trailer that leaks rainwater down around the rivets. Louie says he'll fix it, but never does. He just now disappeared under the trailer pretending to check something. Actually, he has a bottle hidden in one of the wheel wells. I don't need to look.

In a minute he'll be knocking on the door to take me in the wheelbarrow to my first show. We move slow because of Louie's wooden leg. Teenie told me he had a good-looking leg once—a prosthesis—but lost it in a card game. The winner had two good legs of his own and didn't need Louie's. What he wanted was to see Louie crawl away.

Before going to the tank we'll stop off at the Menagerie so I can scratch Jambal's ears. Jambal has ears the size of Louie's hands and paws like snowshoes. Teenie said he's the biggest circus lion in the world. When he sees us coming he rolls over on his back and closes his eyes, I guess to better enjoy the experience.

Teenie said that families and home are one and the same. Without a family there's no home to go back to.

Like dust, I drift from set-up to tear-down feeling the same emptiness in between. I really shouldn't complain. Jambal needs me, and so does Louie.

ANGEL OF SCALDED CREEK

CHASTITY WAS A PULCHRITUDINOUS WOMAN IN THAT OVERLY TITTED hillbilly style. Her upper arm flab was offset by the yellow hair set firm and airy as chicken wire, the eye shadow bulldozed into levees around liquid blue ponds, the lavender scent trailing like a bass just under the surface of nausea. All told, she was her own best advertisement for the unlicensed beauty parlor that she operated alone out of her doublewide.

One morning in spring she swung open the front door and smiled down at an archipelago of crabgrass patterning the hardscrabble yard. Glass shards littered the barren interstices, beaming greenly. Seated on her doorstep, coffee cup balanced on nightgowned knees, Chastity heard a bobwhite in the distance, and its voice made her marvel aloud at God's handiwork. The barking dogs and crowing roosters, the flatulent coal trucks crawling up the mountain, were additional liminal delights, evidence of His miracles. In her own eyes she was an Angel of the Morning as sung by the Pretenders, and a passerby might wonder why she was smiling. She sang softly to herself, *Just call me angel of the morning, Angel/ Just touch my cheek/Before you leave me, baby...*

He did in fact wonder, leaning stoned at sunrise into the flat shadows, conscious of his own stink. He considered that she was either retarded or a guileless figment of the ether somehow exiled to Hell. Such childish happiness was unnatural. The Quaalude he'd taken an hour before had not altered his vision, bombarded as it was by ugliness. Everything around seemed real; that was the problem. He patted his shirt pocket, sensing the ghost of a cigarette packet. Grasping a corner of the trailer for support, he took inventory of what he owned, actual or imagined. The list was not long: a bum's clothes and what remained of a hard-on.

Seeking the light's warmth, he now stepped forward, only to fall sprawling at Chastity's feet. He was wet all over, having slipped into the creek earlier while taking a piss. Strange, he thought, that she didn't run inside to call the cops. He lay still, trying to remember a reason to move. Loose stones pushed against his ribs; underneath the trailer a yellow cat hissed and withdrew farther into the darkness. He rolled onto his back and saw Chastity staring at him. She handed down her coffee cup and said that what he needed was a shower, a shave, and some breakfast. He had never in all his life heard anything so sensible.

Unknown to him, he was the fulfillment of a prophecy. Chastity, as a child of ten, had been visited by an angel who advised her to save herself for one of God's messengers. It was summertime and she was sitting on a rock, dangling her feet in Scalded Creek and wishing she were a mermaid. The angel had soggy wings and seemed distracted, as if late for a job interview. He also forgot to mention exactly who would be showing up—him, or another angel, or whatever. His visit had occurred before computers so there was no celestial record of Chastity's virginal equity having already been cashed in. Just the previous week Poppa's younger brother, Uncle Suede, had forced her thin bones down on top of the cellar coal pile, ripping her only Sunday dress and staining the white ruffles black. Seeing the damage, Mama had lifted those ruffles and whipped her calves with a willow switch. The recollection of it still stung. Eighteen years was a long time to wait.

Traditionally, angels are airborne creatures, but to Chastity there remained a definite link with water. The vision of the angel at the creek and her yearning to become a mermaid merged parabiotically into an angel with a fish's tail. And in this form the image remained. For a long time she found herself stopping at puddles to stir them with her toe, or chinning herself on fence railings to see into farm ponds, or peering intently down the shitholes of outhouses. She even inspected half-full coffee cups and empty RC Cola bottles, having been told by someone about miniature angels. Her behavior near water remained such a lasting oddity that inhabitants of Scalded Creek no longer noticed.

While he slept, Chastity washed and dried his clothes, ironed them, and hung them over the chair beside the bed. By the time he emerged, yawning and stretching, she was dressed in skin-tight jeans and a tight sweater, and he forgot momentarily about needing a wake-up cigarette and a glass of Scotch.

She served up a supper of pork chops with fried potatoes and corn bread, noticing that the pupils of his eyes seemed depthless, widening instead of narrowing in the light, actively drawing her in until all barriers of safety fell away. He seemed less distracted than before. She watched him eat, astonished at her feelings, wondering if he could still fly.

In truth he had barely survived the trip. There had been no destination, no memory even of departing, just the Pennsylvania Turnpike and rumors of spring. At a diner south of Pittsburgh a trucker saw him muttering into his coffee and offered a ride. The man spoke an unfamiliar hill dialect. Drunk and homesick for his personal subway grate. He misunderstood, taking the destination for West End Avenue or maybe the West Side Highway rather than West Virginia.

The driver let him out at dawn on a road that rolled sideways and twisted back on itself like a car-struck snake. The MetLife Building was nowhere in sight. He discarded the remnants of his jacket and started walking. All around were trees newly leafed and green. Old women rocked on swaybacked porches in the company of loafing hounds. There were gnats and horseflies, cows even. My God! The wildlife! Where the land flattened briefly its soil bore signs of cultivation. A herd of deer moved across the road, backlit by the morning sun, and way off, rising from the mist like a steaming slag heap, lay the coal camp of Scalded Creek.

As he chewed he glanced around at a portrait of Jesus looking pale and anglicized, at needlepoint homilies framed and mounted, and considered his options. To a moral indigent as yet uninvested in the hereafter, it seemed like a good moment to turn Christian. Preaching was at least as interesting as otorhinolaryngology or hippopotamology. The scripture's quaint poetry had long held appeal, and he could call up certain passages with ease. He grinned largely and forked another chop onto his plate.

He told her his name was Stephen, which maybe it was. His voice had an adolescent's high pitch and sustained excitement, and the effect was oddly contagious. St. Stephen had been a martyr and a saint, he told her, and quoted from Acts: *Stephen, a man full of faith and of the Holy Ghost . . . did great wonders and miracles among the people.* Her eyes grew wide and she got up to fetch the coffee pot. He envisioned her mind nibbling at the words, wary as a rabbit on short grass. Aha! And a saint, no less! Pushing back the chair, he stood brandishing a pork chop bone and said: *And they stoned Stephen, calling upon God, and saying, Lord Jesus, receive my spirit.*

Having been personally stoned most of his adult life, it was a modest opening performance delivered from the heart. The perpendicularity of Chastity's bosom and the splay of her haunch supplied its own vision. *I love you,* he lied. Instantly she was atop him *à cheval,* moaning and probing his scapulae for vestiges of wings.

The Holiness church where she took him that evening was an unpainted frame structure stuck against a hillside, a five-minute walk from her trailer. Gallused men waiting to pray turned towards them. On seeing Chastity they shuffled nervously and tried to look away, eyeing her sweater sideways as the starving dog eyes a steak.

Inside the building were cobwebs and a scent of mold. The earthen floor was packed hard under a patina of dust, its center dished to a lower elevation by tramping feet. A platform extended across the end of the building opposite the door. On the platform was a pulpit consisting of a board straddling rough timbers, covered now with a checkered tablecloth.

The preacher, a balding man gone to paunch, adjusted his suspenders and said, *Allow me, Jesus, to quote from the Gospel according to Mark. Y'all listen now and hear His holy Word.* He opened the Bible as the listeners fidgeted and coughed themselves to silence. *And these signs shall follow them that believe: In my name shall they cast out devils; they shall speak with new tongues; They shall take up serpents; and if they drink any deadly thing, it shall not hurt them; they shall lay hands on the sick, and they shall recover.*

The preacher leaned on the pulpit and said in a conspiratorial voice, *I went out in the woods last week to pray. Makes a person feel closer to God, wilderness does, oh yes. Jesus prayed there. Good enough for him, good enough for me. A'course I couldn't of lasted 40 days.* He smiled toothlessly and patted his stomach. The congregation laughed. He raised up off his elbows and looked around the room, cocking an ear towards the back as if anticipating something, but everything was quiet.

Save him, Jesus! a woman shouted. There was a stirring, a disturbance of the dust under their shoes like a swift deep current.

He whispered to his audience, *I've got the name of Jesus tucked next to my heart like this here hankie.* He produced a handkerchief and with a flourish tucked it inside his shirt. *But Jesus, he lives inside my heart, not outside! Right here!* He thumped his chest.

The people answered, *Praise to you, God! Hear him, Lord!* They stamped and shook. *Watch over him, Jesus!* they cried.

The preacher continued, *I have a friend in Jesus, don't you? Amen, say it, brother!*

I've let Jesus into my heart, into my soul. I feel him, I feel him here! The preacher grabbed the front of his shirt and bunched it into a fist. He dragged himself across the platform with a hop and a step and stood himself upright. The fist relaxed, becoming a hand that patted down the wrinkles. *I'm not ashamed to say I fear the Lord's might! I ain't afraid to say it: I'm a sinner! Yessir, a sinner! Please, Lord. Please deliver me from Satan! Lord, I have need of you!* The preacher fell to his knees, a hank of hair dangling from the side of his bald pate, his shoulders heaving.

A rotund man rushed forward. He reached under the altar and turned grinning, a live rattler in each hand. He danced a brief jig then draped the snakes around his neck. Another man made a show of producing a small plastic bag of white powder and dusting his lips. Stephen moved to get some thinking it was coke, but Chastity held him back. She cupped a hand to his ear and whispered, *Strychnine.*

Bless Jesus! Bless His holy name! exclaimed the man seated beside Stephen. He turned, not unkindly. *Testify, brother,* he said. The congregation, risen as one, abandoned the benches. *Hear him, Lord! Thank you God for Jesus!* There was no choreographing the waving arms, the shouting; no subtlety. Then came music. People alone or in twos and threes gathered at the middle of the room. Tambourines rattled, punctuating cymbals clashed like metal pans dropped in a scullery. From a tall stool the hunching guitarist worried his strings, pausing once to turn up the volume on his amplifier. Individual noises reminiscent of the subway, a disco, sunrise at the Bronx Zoo, merged cacophonously, the unified shriek of demons being driven from the walls and floor. Stephen downed a 'lude and climbed onto the platform.

My name is Stephen, he said. *St. Stephen got stoned for his beliefs, but me, I get stoned for not having any, praise be to Jesus! I used to be a sinner—a drinker and a fornicator, a wastrel.* He didn't tell them that he still was. *I was a marketer, a creator and mover of product in that great Sodom, New York City, until happiness became elusive. I showed you products you didn't need and convinced you to want them. I took from you, from your children, and made all of you poor. Then they took from me, and I too became impoverished. No fault of mine.* He looked down at the out-of-focus faces. *The sunny world of happiness turned dark as it came around; the big red ball ceased to shine.* He chuckled in that high uneasy voice, and people drew closer.

I got tossed in the drunk tank. There I lectured fellow inmates about the city as insatiable organism, themselves as replaceable cells. Nobody understood anything he said; his voice was carrying them. He omitted how most inmates had ignored him or told him to shut the fuck up, but that some gathered listening. *Apoptosis!* he had yelled. *Programmed cell death! It's a conspiracy!* He didn't mention how at the arraignment he asked to be represented by a Jew, preferably Alan Greenspan or Sandy Koufax, and served three days. *Time enough,* he now shouted, *to await the stone soon rolled away!* Upon hearing this allusion to angels, Chastity shivered.

Did it work? Stephen screamed. *Did that experience cure me? No, brothers and sisters, it did not! I lived in squalor. My roommates were bedbugs and roaches, my neighbors prostitutes, failed scam artists, petty thieves, pickpockets with shaking hands, drug-addicted artists and poets, tired waitresses, drunks. I stopped buying razor blades and soap and forgot where I lived, waking often with my cheek pressed to the sidewalk and ceasing to be astonished when the streets stank like puke after rain. Once I awoke to a wet tongue licking my face. The tongue paused at my ear and said, Honey, you wouldn't mind sharing some of that bottle you're laying on, now would you?*

The church vibrated as people writhed and jerked to their private muses, getting the Holy Spirit. They reached out and touched him, and he leaned into the crowd lurching and swaying as if balancing on a moving train. Some worshippers knelt and prayed silently or not so silently; some wept and rejoiced or simply stood there uttering incomprehensible sounds. A few fell to the floor twitching and moaning. Still others dropped to their knees and weaved back and forth like rearing caterpillars. *Jesus loves you!* he told them. And they believed him.

In days following Stephen bucked her frontways and caudad, before morning canzonets on the trailer steps and in the grim afternoons. To the pitching headboard he bayed verses from Ecclesiastes, reaffirming his newly acquired sainthood: *Go not after thy lusts, but refrain thyself from thine appetites!*

Chastity lost her singing voice but gained sustained nipple erections. After a month she threw away the Thighmaster and vitamin pills. When she worried that God condemns the fornicator, he quoted, *Again, if two lie together, then they have heat: but how can one be warm alone?* She pointed out that it was practically summer, and with those hair dryers going the trailer was getting hotter than you-know-where. He replied that winter was hiding somewhere plotting its return, and anyway, the observation had come from Ecclesiastes and he was just passing it along.

She sniffled that she could never have children, naming an obscure uterine malady peculiar to her lineage. Unenticed anyway by lactating hooters, he answered with some relief that God moved in peculiar ways.

He told her about his own dear child, furrowing his brow to recall invented generalities, turning to face her in the sorrowful trailer light and pretending to hold back the rest. So sad are they upon growing up and gaining moral sicknesses and disappointments of their own. The remembrances families emboss on their young: call these elements love or apathy; even worse, forgiveness. He shook his head. Yes, little one, I cared. Go forth now to carve out your very own piece of Earth and fuck it over. Be fruitful and multiply despite the true need of our species: a genetic bottleneck narrower than your average epididymis.

Being a father seemed so sad. She cried and told him that more men should have his sensitivity.

As summer swelled, Scalded Creek shrank to a narrow ribbon of suspended coal dust, its torpid eddies trod by melancholy water striders. Twigs formed dams across its riffles, reinforced with condoms and beer cans and plastered over by sodden toilet paper from the shithouses upstream. Stephen helped around the beauty parlor, carrying sacks of hair clippings outside to the mulch pile, sweeping up, arranging magazines, replacing fuses. He knelt and prayed with Chastity's clients before they took to the chairs, being available afterwards for advice on all matters, including what to expect from your average multiple orgasm and whether eating too much squirrel could make a man go soft. The women thanked him tearfully.

The preacher gave him his head in church, where he showed evidence of being touched by the Holy Ghost. He spoke in tongues and might even have drunk from the jar of strychnine water kept on the pulpit beside the Bible. He learned to handle angry rattlers, being careful not to be first to reach into the box. It was only a matter of time, he figured, before he could cast out demons and heal the sick. Once, under a particularly violent anointing, he jumped out a window, landing on a pile of wet dog turds before rolling with a yelp into the greenbriars. The preacher reminded him later that faith isn't always enough, and that to take up serpents— one of the five signs following—you must never doubt your anointing by the Holy Ghost. God might let a snake bite you as a test of your faith, and if you died it could be because you were a backslider not worthy of His salvation.

Stephen's influence grew, flowering fully one Sunday night in August. Everyone in Scalded Creek had gathered in the church. The preacher ended his opening monologue, and the Lord was just starting to move on the congregation. A few chords struck by the guitar player alerted the tambourine shakers and cymbalist. They were his prompts too.

He stood suddenly in front of the pulpit looking rapturous, beard and hair long and black, arms open in a crucifixion mode. Blood oozed from his palms where nail holes could have been. Actually, it was mail-order blood from an abattoir packaged in gelatin capsules that he deftly twisted apart. A little EDTA had been added by the supplier to prevent clots from forming, and in the dimness his borrowed humanity oozed blackly as if cued by providence.

The eyes and ears of the watchers—women, mostly—were diverted from any sleight of hand. Submerged in delusional ecstasy they watched as God manipulated the trembling mouth; they saw flashing sclera in the rolled-back eyes, a barely perceptible shimmy finding rhythm in the Holy Word. His staccato glossolalia filled spaces between guitar chords, signifying everything and nothing, rising thickly like chrism through water music—or, as some later believed, Christ ascending. Into this chaos fell the spent capsules, invisible as flies, which he ground into the dirt floor.

Ashes to ashes, gelatin to dust.

Women clutched his legs, feeling in worn denim an enlightened man of ignorant cloth, a rapacious new Jesus. Some swooned, lying immobile as if tied to train tracks and awaiting the onrush of Salvation. Dusty now, slathered with sweat, the preacher knelt and attended his sinful flock, assessing on a continuum of youth and bra size the heavenly value of their souls.

Stephen noticed none of this, content with his role as a solipsist among primitives, or maybe a high priest of orgasmic disco. Among the unexpected swooners that night was Chastity. When the preacher's hands reached under her arms, squeezing her breasts together and forcing the cleavage into shadow, she was heard to shout, *Is that you, Jesus?* And the preacher shouted back, *Yes, my child, and although the hands are mine it's God who directs them to these holy parts. Praise His name!* And Chastity answered, *Hallelujah to Glory! I see her standing among us! I see her spreading wings, her fishy tail!*

Then Stephen had no choice except to look down, aware suddenly of his own real blood ready to spurt through every orifice and even the pores of his skin. Product development had moved on him, and he felt anointed by the power of Marketing.

Chastity's vision was transmitted instantly to everyone, as if he had become the conduit that linked them. Of those still standing, all except Stephen fell to their knees, pointing up and speaking in tongues. A scaly angel sculled somewhere overhead, dripping real water onto the congregation. The possibility of a leaky roof could be eliminated; rain had not fallen for weeks over that part of West Virginia and Kentucky, as CNN was later to report. An angel had indeed appeared: the Angel of Scalded Creek.

Stephen stood twitching, feeling the many hands. He too pictured wings and the tail of a fish, except made in thermosetting plastic of virginal white, manufactured in Manila or Taiwan and shipped in bulk.

His own specific visions were of angels vaguely resembling Chastity—fully-titted and wearing big hair and jeans, of height maybe four inches: one model with a ring for hanging from a rear-view mirror, the other having a suction cup underneath the tail for sticking on a dashboard. Super-imposed over these was an image of himself with arms out-stretched and head tilted back, shining bright and golden as an epaulet. That model could come along later.

After the ensuing publicity, letters enclosing money poured into Chastity's mail box at the Scalded Creek Post Office. There was so much mail the postmaster started handing it to her over the counter in cardboard boxes. Big-city reporters camped for days in her front yard, cursing the broken glass and pissing in the creek. The United Mine Workers Union stood guard with squirrel guns outside the church to keep Catholics from sneaking in and prospecting for religious arti-facts, such as the occasional broken scale or bent feather, even water droplets.

HBO filmed a documentary on Southern Pentecostal churches, emphasizing the taking up of serpents and drinking of strychnine. Citizens of Scalded Creek came shuf-fling voluntarily or were dragged into the camera lights to tes-tify. They attributed many miracles to Stephen, including healing by the laying on of hands, levitation, and raising of the dead, none of which he either openly acknowledged or denied. Stephen was interviewed extensively, and there was even talk of his own TV show on a competing channel oppo-site Oprah Winfrey. The working title "Angel Droppings" was Chastity's idea. The show would feature testimonies of ordi-nary people who had been visited by the Angel of Scalded Creek. Unfortunately, their sponsors backed out.

Angel sightings were reported from Roswell, New Mexico, and elsewhere across America, most descriptions including mention of a fish tail and dripping water even during droughts. An artist's rendering of the Angel of Scalded Creek appeared on a cover of *Newsweek*. Chastity had been consulted as the work progressed and was quoted as saying that the final art represented her visions, more or less. A professor of aerospace engineering at Cal Tech published a scientific paper demonstrating how angels without tails would be aerodynamically unstable, prone to crashing in the least bit of turbulence, and that a fish's tail might be the perfect appendage for both stability and abrupt changes of direction while in flight.

The beauty parlor was closed, the chairs and hair dryers replaced by fax machines and computers, desks and file cabinets. Stephen re-established credit in New York and ordered in a large supply of Quaaludes. In an effort to maintain good Christian balance, he had recently relinquished strong drink and embraced jug wine, using as inspiration the Book of Proverbs: *Give . . . wine unto those that be of heavy hearts. Let him drink, and forget his poverty, and remember his misery no more.* Some of the donations were invested in a Napa Valley vineyard as a hedge against lean times. The Angel of Scalded Creek became a copyrighted trademark. A New York lawyer prepared legal documents making Angel of Scalded Creek Productions a religious nonprofit corporation doing business as The Holiness Church of Roadside Temptation Passing By.

Not surprisingly, life in Scalded Creek changed forever. Chastity and Stephen traveled most of the time, evangelizing and raising money. Chastity's uterus eventually untangled of its own accord and she conceived, no small miracle itself. Stephen's son ran away from boarding school in Houston and joined them, claiming to be sick of living in high humidity without a swimming pool. In publicity photos he's the onanistic lad with damp hands and toggling ears. Sometimes he leads the choir.

Their revival is still going strong. Stop at a diner anywhere— McDowell, Oceana, Stollings, Jolo, even as far north as Charleston—it doesn't matter. Ask the waitress for a brochure and schedule of events, or walk over to the post office and look on the bulletin board. Everyone knows about the Angel of Scalded Creek.

TASTE JUST LIKE MOA

In his green valley infested by moas, Tuta Patahuri the Maori awoke and decided to go fishing. As chief of the village, he could go fishing whenever he felt like it.

Tuta Patahuri rolled partway over on his sleeping mat and felt beside him for his wife, but she was already outside preparing his breakfast of fernroot. He heard her grunting as she pounded the fernroot to separate meal from fiber, heard the slap of her hands as she shaped the meal cakes for roasting in *te hangi*, her oven in the ground. He pictured sighing flab looking oiled in the early sunlight, sweat hissing as it fell onto the red-hot stones, and considered the unfairness of a Maori proverb about female shapeliness: "Massage the legs of your daughter, that she may have a good appearance when standing naked before a fire on the beach."

Tuta Patahuri lay still, sniffing in the aroma of roasting fernroot. Kirikiri's mournful notes floated to him from where the seashore and river met. Kirikiri's single passion was music. He could sit hours at a time under a palm beside the sea blowing into his *pu-moana*, a sort of trumpet consisting of a large seashell with a wooden mouthpiece attached at one end. What was it with kids and music? Tuta Patahuri lay quietly listening to Kirikiri's monotonous notes, to murmuring voices from the village and the distant crowing of moas. Tuta Patahuri scratched his balls vigorously, then sat up and yawned.

"Today I go fishing for *kahawai*," he announced to his wife.

"Good," she replied. "Take Kirikiri with you. His *pu-moana* is driving me nuts."

"I'd rather take Tamati, your brother," Tuta Patahuri answered. "He's almost as worthless as Kirikiri, but at least he doesn't throw up in the canoe."

"Take them both," said his wife. She sounded bored, or maybe hot from bending over *te hangi*. He pictured her squatting beside the pit, legs thick and lumpy as tree trunks, and thought he could detect in the cooking smoke an odor of unwashed woman.

Tuta Patahuri, who seldom was charitable, felt so today. "So be it," he said, then added, "I'll make them into men yet. 'All honor those who have been baptized in the waters of the war god.'" His wife grunted contemptuously.

With a heave, Tuta Patahuri separated his great bulk from the ground and in two thunderous steps stood in the entrance of his hut. With a balletic move, he lifted one foot and farted loudly. "Is there meat?" he asked.

Without turning, his wife answered, "You ate all there was last night. A whole leg, remember? One nearly as large as your own."

Tuta Patahuri rubbed his stomach and considered. Yes, the evidence lay off to the side of *te hangi*: leg bones scattered in the dirt along with remnants of a gnawed tarsus. It was time to raid a neighboring village. His own was running short of long pig.

"It makes you flatulent," his wife remarked.

"What does?"

"Long pig. It's too rich. The next day all you do is fart."

"You're jealous," he said, a reminder that the eating of human flesh by women was *tapu*.

She retrieved his roasted fernroot from beneath an earth-covered mat set over the hot stones, saying, "Here's your breakfast. I have laundry waiting." Then she stood and waddled off towards the river.

While he ate, Tuta Patahuri listened to Kirikiri play the *pu-moana* and was overcome with good feeling. It was during this very month fifteen years ago that he had slain Hapara Nihoniho, his wife's first cousin, and feasted on his flesh.

After finishing breakfast and licking his fingers, Tuta Patahuri retrieved from a corner of the hut Hapara Nihoniho's pre-
served head. He lifted it by the hair and held it to the light. A
good job, he thought. Tuta Patahuri remembered how, after
snacking on the eyeballs and tongue, he had cut off the head
and extracted its brain by enlarging the hole at the base of
the skull. He had then stretched the skin of the neck and
sewn it to a hoop of stiff vine. Afterwards, he wrapped the
head in green leaves and placed it for a time in *te hangi*
before curing it slowly over smoke.

Today, he told the head, we go fishing, you and I, and dis-
cuss silently how you stole my slender wife and made her
pregnant with Kirikiri, and how when I got her back she grew
fat as a sow and has stayed that way. My wife wept as she
flayed the meat from your bones; tears flowed like the river
as she roasted your flesh in *te hangi* for my victory feast!
Even now she holds your head between her sagging breasts
and weeps on the occasion of your birthday. Hapara Nihoniho, I must confess, I enjoyed lunching on you immensely,
but on the subject of wife-stealing I perhaps judged you too
harshly. He chuckled and belched.

"Kirikiri!" he bellowed. "Stop making noise and collect the
fishing gear. We're going out. Tell Tamati he's coming with
us." Then he set off along the main path through the village
to round up men to paddle the canoe so he could troll for
kahawai.

From the storehouse at the center of the village he collected
his fishing line made of twisted flax, his stone sinkers, and his
special lure, a fishhook carved from one of Hapara Nihoniho's
ribs and faced with iridescent shell so that it flashed like a
silvery baitfish in the undersea light. Tied around the front of
the lure were tail feathers from a blue penguin. *Kahawai*
found the combination irresistible. The turning of one's enemy into a fishing lure degraded his memory, and Tuta
Patahuri had taken exquisite pleasure in fashioning this one.

Kirikiri arrived at the river beside the fish weir where canoes
were tethered to palms leaning out from the shore. "Carry
your father," Tuta Patahuri told him, and thrust the head

against his chest. Kirikiri, a slight boy with intelligent eyes, seemed pained. He will not grow, thought Tuta Patahuri, without ever eating meat. Boys do not become men on a diet of fernroot and sow-thistle. And his wife condoned this!

"Did you have to bring it?" asked Kirikiri.

"Yes, of course," Tuta Patahuri replied. "And the fishing lure, also named Hapara Nihoniho. Lures made from human bones must always be named."

"I'll get seasick, and everyone will laugh at me," Kirikiri said.

Tuta Patahuri shrugged. 'Slippery or uncertain is the fame of the warrior,'" he answered, quoting another Maori proverb. He looked at Tamati, who might have been Kirikiri's twin except for his greater bulk. "And you?"

"I won't throw up," Tamati said.

"Good! We leave now." Everyone clambered aboard, and the canoe shoved off.

On that morning Hapara Nihoniho, the fishing lure, was devastating, hooking a *kahawai* almost as soon as he began his simulated swim. By afternoon the bottom of the canoe was filled with gasping fish, and the paddlers were tired from pushing their vessel fashioned from a heavy log through the glistening swells. Kirikiri smiled because he had paddled all morning without being sick. Everyone else laughed and smiled because the trip would soon end. They were hungry and wished to return to the village. The carrying of food aboard a fishing canoe was *tapu*. Even Hapara Nihoniho, the head, seemed contented, swinging gaily by his hair from an outrigger.

"Paddle faster," Tuta Patahuri admonished them. "We must catch the king of *kahawai*." With a groan the weary crew responded, and the canoe seemed to plane across the troughs of the swells. Suddenly Hapara Nihoniho, the lure, stuck fast, and the flax line cut through Tuta Patahuri's fingers, causing blood to drip onto his substantial knees.

"Stop paddling!" he shouted. "The king has been hooked!" He gradually pulled in the line, playing the lure so as not to lose it in the mouth of the fish, letting line out when the tension became too great, pulling in when there was slack. An hour passed. The canoe drifted away from land, although the land could be located easily by the long white cloud that hung above it.

The crew members rested. They discussed the coming raid on a nearby village and how sweet their enemy's flesh would taste. They talked about pinning the women to the earthen floors of the huts by driving wooden stakes through their feet, keeping them alive while the victors feasted on their husbands, brothers, and children. Afterwards, the women would be taken to wife before being slaughtered. They hoped the raid would happen soon because they were bored with eating only fish and moa. Kirikiri and Tamati, who ate no meat at all, were silent.

The blue feathers of Hapara Nihoniho, the lure, appeared suddenly beside them, and everyone gazed in astonishment. Hooked through the upper lip was a sea maiden, exhausted now from her struggle. She lay panting at the surface, her slender tail fanning feebly. In size she was like a girl of twelve or thirteen with small breasts and long flowing hair. The large yellow eyes were lidless, the upper torso smooth and like a human's, except iridescent blue on the back and sides and silvery below. From the waist down she was scaled in similar hues.

"We take this fish home," Tuta Patahuri said. He put a heavy arm around her and lifted her aboard, but she promptly slithered from his grasp and began to thrash among the dying fish.

"This fish is slippery like the rest," Tuta Patahuri muttered. "But it will die without water. We must fill our canoe with the sea." The crew picked up their human skulls used as bailers and began shipping seawater aboard until there was enough depth for the sea maiden to submerge her head.

The canoe wallowed back to the river's mouth. Fortunately the tide was coming in, which made paddling a little easier. It was dark when they arrived and tied up, and everyone except Tuta Patahuri was exhausted. The party divided up the *kahawai* and everyone trudged slowly home. Tuta Patahuri picked up his sea maiden, now gasping in the foul water at the bottom of the canoe, and tossed her into the fish weir for the night. There was no means of escape after he had blocked the entrance with a gate of saplings anchored by stones and secured it tightly with flax rope.

The next morning everyone in the village gathered at the fish weir to gape at the sea maiden. Even newborn babies were held above the heads of their mothers to gain a better view.

"What will you do with her?" asked Tuta Patahuri's wife.

"Feed her fish," he replied.

"But our village needs the weir for catching fish."

"Then the men of our village can build another," Tuta Patahuri said, and walked away to catch baitfish for his sea maiden, which was now swimming in a circle at the surface and appeared to be hungry.

That night Tuta Patahuri ordered Kirikiri to stop spending all day on the beach blowing into his *pu-moana* and start catching baitfish for the sea maiden. "Unlike you," he said, "she can't exist on a diet of fernroot and sow-thistle. She needs flesh from the sea to keep her strong and supple."

The next day and for many subsequent days Tuta Patahuri and Kirikiri caught baitfish, which they threw into the weir. The sea maiden took them with joyous splashing. Gradually she became tame, and they fed her by hand. Upon hearing the voice of either Tuta Patahuri or Kirikiri, she swam to the shore side of the weir, raised her head out of water despite the oppression of air, and extended her hands palms up to receive fish. Small fishes were gulped headfirst; larger ones she tore apart and swallowed a piece at a time with minimal chewing.

On a morning after sending Kirikiri away to catch more bait-fish, Tuta Patahuri disrobed. Entering the weir, he frolicked with his sea maiden, who swam around him in a teasing manner, ducking away before he could grab her. When he returned to the hut for his midday meal, his wife noticed that he was wet.

"Did you fall into the water?" she asked.

"I was swimming with the sea maiden," he replied. "I'm thinking of taking her to wife."

"Taking her to *wife*? But she's half fish, and in case you

haven't noticed, it's the wifely half that's the fish." She shook her head and went to the river to do the laundry.

There must be a way, thought Tuta Patahuri, unless fishes are the ones who take sea maidens to wife. But no, she was half human. Aha! he said to himself. She's obviously a daughter of *Marakihau*, the giant sea monster who sucks up canoes filled with warriors through his tubular tongue. *Marakihau* has the upper torso of a human and the ass end of a fish. He went to the river to find his wife.

"This one is too small to be a daughter of *Marakihau*," his wife said while watching the sea maiden frolic in the weir. "Unless she's a runt."

"Maybe," Tuta Patahuri replied thoughtfully. "But I'm still taking her to wife." His wife shrugged and picked up her wet laundry.

"Then you expect to lie with me afterwards?"

"Stop complaining," Tuta Patahuri said. "Tell it to Hapara Nihoniho, the head."

The next day Tuta Patahuri sent an emissary to a neighboring village. The emissary took along the village's last basket of smoked long pig and a live lizard. The emissary was given a message to deliver: tell the chief that I, Tuta Patahuri, have taken to wife a daughter of *Marakihau*, and that soon I shall rule the seas all around this great island of *Aotearoa*, land of the long white cloud. Those who join with me in raiding the common enemy not only will feast well on long pig, but benefit by feasting endlessly from the sea. As the son-in-law of *Marakihau*, it can be no other way.

The emissary was not killed and eaten. In fact, he reported back that the chief had consumed the lizard alive, a sign of his commitment, and that soon he would send his own emissary to view this sea maiden personally.

The other chief's emissary came and went, obviously impressed. No one in this part of *Aotearoa* had ever seen a live sea maiden, especially a relative of the terrifying *Marakihau*.

Each day that Tuta Patahuri entered the weir the sea maiden became friendlier, rubbing her cold slimy body against his warm flab, teasing him into erections with her hands that were cold and slippery as eels. He felt her all over but could not find the womanly opening. This he told to his wife.

Tuta Patahuri's wife had become jealous. She replied, "'Only a penis travels under cover of darkness,'" quoting a Maori proverb about uninvited guests who arrive after sunset, a clear reference to the sea maiden. "Don't tell me your troubles, tell them to her," and she left to gather green leaves for cooking the evening meal.

A raid was organized. Tuta Patahuri and his allies, tattooed faces looking fierce, joined after dark and paddled south along the rugged shore of *Aotearoa*. Each war canoe held seventy paddlers, two abreast, dipping their oars in unison to chants given by Tuta Patahuri and lesser chiefs standing amidship. Besides a greenstone club for cracking enemy skulls, every warrior carried a short spear with an obsidian point.

The canoes grounded softly under a new moon, on a high tide that erased all footprints. They caught the sentries asleep and were inside the village before any of the inhabitants awoke. As the Maori proverb goes, "When the eyes of those who fish for eels are sleeping, the eyes of those who catch mullet are open."

The carnage was total. By dawn, the enemy warriors were dead, and many had been dismembered and flayed for roasting. The butchering was done by women of the village, and in days following they were taken to wife before being eaten.

After a week, Tuta Patahuri and his warriors returned to their own village triumphant, bearing heavy baskets of human flesh and sweet potatoes dug from the enemy's fields. As son-in-law of *Marakihau*, Tuta Patahuri was now feared and respected all along the coast. There would be no problem securing allies for future raids when this batch of long pig was consumed.

"Here are more of your relatives," Tuta Patahuri said to his wife, and swung a heavy basket to the ground. "Smoke them properly. I see now that obesity travels in your family like fish of a school."

"And in yours," she replied. "You don't appear to have skipped any meals lately." Tuta Patahuri ignored her sarcasm. "Send Kirikiri and Tamati to clean out the canoes."

"They've gone away. They left our village and went north to live with relatives of mine, who are more civilized than yours. They intend to be musicians, playing the *kouau* and *pu-moana* together."

"The *kouau*?" asked Tuta Patahuri, who possessed no musical talent.

"A flute," said his wife. "Tamati made it from a thigh bone you tossed into the bushes."

"Is there more to this story about a flute?" Tuta Patahuri asked irritably. "How will they live?"

"It won't be hard. They don't eat long pig or moa, not even fish. Sow-thistle and fernroot are easy to come by, taking little effort. They can concentrate on playing their music. The other young people like it. They close their eyes while listening, and the girls often scream as if possessed. Musicians have many wives."

Tuta Patahuri shook his head, unable to comprehend how any male Maori could refuse long pig, his favorite dish. "So they don't wish to be warriors?"

"They wish to play music, to sing and dance."

"'With testicles an erection can be sustained,'" Tuta Patahuri quoted. "These young men have no balls."

"So you say," his wife answered. "Let's look out back."

Puzzled, Tuta Patahuri walked around behind his hut and saw a pile of bones and fish scales. Some of the scales were bluish, others silvery. Hanging over a smoldering fire, suspended by the hair, was the head of his sea maiden.

He turned to his wife. "You ate my sea maiden?"

"You ate my other husband," his wife replied.

"Now you've eaten a daughter of *Marakihau* before I could take her to wife! Have you nothing to say for doing this stupid thing?"

His wife grinned. "Taste just like moa," she answered.

OLD WOMAN FRAMED AND BACKLIT

WE CAME TOGETHER ON A COLD NIGHT OF TENUOUS WIND. Trees swayed blackly overhead and snow lay in glittering screes against the curbs and stone façades. Dusty snowflakes had collected like dander on the shoulders of her tattered coat. The stoop, the shuffling steps made her seem ancient. Her hair had recently been wet. It was matted, the ends straight and frozen.

"I've been waiting for you," she said in a voice without reproach or complaint.

"I meant to come sooner," I replied, and led her to my single room across the street.

I helped her along the dim corridor, careful to see that her shoes, which were sturdy and of an antiquated design, did not catch in the threadbare carpet. The hall was narrow. When we reached the door to my room, I nudged her gently towards the opposite wall so that I could insert the key in the lock.

After opening the door and stepping inside, I beckoned her to follow. She hesitated, framed in the doorway and backlit, her face in shadow. "Is this correct?" she asked.

"Yes," I answered.

"Then we can begin." Without further hesitation she stepped across the threshold. I switched on my desk lamp, and when I turned again to face her she was blinking back the light. Her eyes were two bright coals set in a furrowed face, her lips like the orifice of a damp internal organ exposed suddenly to the dry air.

"May I take your coat?"

"No, I'll keep it. On such a cold night a person can't warm up properly even indoors."

"Please sit down," I said, indicating an armchair beside my desk. She was short—tiny, actually—and when she sat her feet did not quite reach the floor, giving her the strange appearance of a wizened child.

I took off my own coat and scarf, shook away the snow, and hung them behind the door. I shucked my wet boots by forcing heel to toe. My wool socks were damp, but not wet, and would soon dry in the heat of the room.

"At last," I said, sitting down at my desk and picking up notebook and pencil. I scraped the chair around to face her. "Sorry for the delay."

"No apology is necessary," she replied evenly. The slight lisp in her speech and the mannerism of working her lips continuously as if sucking on a straw were probably caused by ill-fitting false teeth. I made a quick note, hoping my observation had been surreptitious.

"My false teeth don't fit right," she said, just as I finished writing. "They told me down at the clinic I could get them fixed, or maybe the State would buy me new ones. But I don't want new ones. Too many trips downtown on the bus to see the dentist. I'd rather keep these."

"I'm sure you can do what you want." My low lamp forced a circle of light onto the desk top. It was now I who was backlit. Except for a digital clock blinking from the kitchen counter, everything was in shadow.

"I haven't yet put this into my story," I said. "Would you feel better if I omitted it?"

"No, why should I care whether you mention false teeth? I'm an old woman, vanity means nothing to me now. Once I was young and beautiful, and when I walked on the beach at Atlantic City the boys trailed along like a pack of hounds. I was always coming out of the sea and pushing back my hair.

I dripped water everywhere. They joked and said I must be a mermaid and that soon my hair would turn green as seaweed, my legs would become a fish's tail. The boys told me this long ago. I can't remember their faces, just their words. Everyone grows old. Maybe even mermaids."

"Excuse me," I said and wrote furiously for several minutes, trying to remember her words verbatim. "That was quite a soliloquy," I remarked when I had finished. "And quite an intimate one, after a fashion."

"What?"

"Quite a speech. I've never heard you reveal so much about yourself," I continued, regretting these words at once. "But please don't stop. I need your words and memories."

"I know," she sighed. "But your writing adds things . . . lies, half-truths. You add to what I say and make me into someone I'm not."

"My imagination does that," I explained. "It dilutes reality with a measure of unreality, guiding human experience onto another level."

She shook her head. "I can't think about those things from my youth. They tear at the few memories I have left. Now you've replaced those with others and stuck them inside me until I'm not me any longer. I can feel you writing me, and your sentences are like evil fingers inside my chest, squeezing my heart."

I set down my pencil and leaned back. There was a moment's pause while she pulled the ends of the faded shawl tied loosely under her chin. "You're a . . . a parasite sucking out my memories and leaving nothing except a shell." Her mouth was working furiously. She grasped the chair arms and pushed herself back, thinking perhaps that she was again sitting in a rocker.

"It can't be helped," I replied, hoping not to sound too abrupt. I consulted my notebook, leafing through the pages until finding the right one. "Your sister was killed by a car when you were six or seven, you don't remember exactly. This sister was your identical twin, and her death left you divided, as if a part of yourself had died too." I tapped the page with my finger to reinforce its veracity. When I looked up she was watching me. Tears formed, one in each coal-black eye, and coursed in synchrony down the furrows of her face.

"My sister drowned," she said. "We were playing by the river. Her body was never found. I don't remember any car accident. If it happened, I wasn't there."

"The story is clear," I insisted. "I've written it. We're here tonight to sort out a few remaining details and inconsistencies. So if you'll bear with me, I can send you along shortly. The last bus stops on the corner at one forty-five."

I settled back and consulted the notebook again. My writing was difficult to read in the dimness, and I turned away from her to better illuminate the pages.

"You and your sister—you've never mentioned her name—were playing on the sidewalk in front of your house. It was summer, an evening in summer, July maybe. There was a crab apple in your front yard, and by your recollection it wasn't in bloom.

"The sultriness is what you recall best, that and insect sounds. And neighborhood noises, of course. Yours was a lower middle class neighborhood, and people had left their windows and doors open for ventilation. You remember laughter. Radios. It was that silver hour of dusk, no longer light but not dark either, the hour when human vision is impaired by insufficient contrast between objects—even moving objects—and the background.

"Your sister said, 'Let's cross the street,' but you refused. You stood stubbornly on the sidewalk looking down at a pair of dirty bare feet, elbows locked, hands clasped behind you, torso twisting negatively back and forth.

"'No!' you shouted. And you remember repeating it: 'No!' Your sister, whom you say was the brave one, the leader, went anyway. Upon reaching the other sidewalk, she turned to taunt you.

"Your anger and frustration rose. In addition, you felt afraid at being left alone, even in front of your own house. Afraid and ashamed of being afraid. And so, you could not give in and relinquish this tiny scrap of independence gained at so great a price. It was a triumph of sorts, a coming out.

"Your sister sensed she had lost control of you and dashed into the street intending to drag you back across with her, if necessary. In her rage she didn't see the car, which appeared suddenly, its headlights not yet turned on. The driver had no time to brake. He told the police he thought he had struck a dog. You watched the scene in horror, not understanding but somehow knowing your life was changed forever.

"With passing years the event took on a surreal quality in which certain physical elements became embellished in memory—the flaxen head of your sister lying on the pavement, white now in the dusk, your parents' wrenching grief, the odd juxtaposition of tears splashing onto the dark fenders of the very instrument of death.

"Later you were asked why you had *let* your sister cross the street alone, the dominance hierarchies of children having been ignored, if considered at all. A reasonable question from an adult's perspective, one placing guilt and shame squarely where they belonged. Couldn't you have taken charge *just once* to avert a tragedy?

"This is all true," I concluded, "because I made it so. Truths and lies evade the permanence of memory with equal facility.

"My story therefore begins, 'She hesitated, framed in the doorway and backlit, her face invisible.' How do you like it?"

I turned back anticipating a response, but the chair was empty. On the floor before it stood a puddle of water. Sunlight streamed through the open window. From the street came smells and sounds of summer. My boots were nowhere in sight, and when I looked behind the door, the coat and scarf were not there either.

THE BLUE ORCHID

THE CURANDERO SAT DOWN ON HIS WOODEN STOOL AND WIPED the sweat from his forehead. He was thin, almost emaciated, and his eyes, recessed within black hollows, seemed out-sized and strangely impassive. His shirt and trousers were filthy, and on his feet were rubber flip-flops. He asked in Spanish if we had brought money.

Bailey, ever the skeptic, turned to me with a snarl. "This guy's a quack."

"That's one definition of *curandero*. The other is witch-doctor," I snapped. We were hot, tired, covered with insect bites, and still five hundred hard miles upriver from civilization.

"I don't see what you hope to gain," Bailey continued. His narrow shoulders slumped more than usual, and his scraggly beard bristled with fatigue and irritation.

"Insight. I hope to gain insight," I hissed back. "The *curanderos* believe life's an illusion—us standing here, the forest, the rivers, the plants and animals. Everything. It's possible to see reality only by riding *yagé*. Tickets are cheap. A trip costs the equivalent of three bucks, and I'm paying Nai-kana's way. He set it up, he's our travel agent. You can't afford it?" Bailey looked past the *curandero* as if willing him to disappear. The idea of getting stoned in such bleak circumstances must have repelled him.

Nai-kana turned his head away and whispered, but the words were directed at me. Bailey, although leader of our three-man expedition, spoke not a word of Spanish.

"He says it's very dangerous," I relayed.

Bailey turned and looked at me, his spectacles glinting in the fading light. "Jungle LSD? Bullshit. But it seems like a needless distraction."

"We have to spend the night somewhere," I reasoned. "Why not here?" When I had mentioned to Nai-kana, our Indian guide, that I wanted to try *yagé*, he told me of the *curandero*. He had imparted the information reluctantly, and his reticence implicitly confirmed what I knew by hearsay; that is, *yagé's* reward might be great, but the experience would surely be unpleasant. I remembered clapping Nai-kana on the shoulder. *Yo sé lo que me hago*, I had said with a laugh. I know what I'm doing.

The *curandero's* hut stood on a knoll in a small clearing. It was a simple frame structure made of poles tied together with lianas, the roof and sides thatched with palm fronds. Living quarters consisted of a bamboo platform raised above ground to protect against snakes, biting insects, and rising water. Somewhere below and out of sight lay the river, where our canoe was tied to the shore.

The *curandero* shouted. His wife appeared immediately in the doorway of the hut. She climbed down the ladder and built up the fire. We gathered around, standing purposely in the smoke hoping to repel the mosquitoes and blackflies. Dusk was always the worst time. Scrabbling noises came from the living quarters. I looked up and saw the *curandero's* children watching us like furtive monkeys through holes in the thatch.

The *curandero* went to the hut and dragged a small table from underneath. He pushed it near the fire, angled it sideways, and set his stool behind it. *Yagé* is a thin pungent liquid prepared by pounding pieces of a liana that has hallucinogenic properties. After soaking in hot water the pulp is strained out and the solution allowed to cool. To the heated preparation a *curandero* sometimes adds the leaves of another liana, *oco-yajé*, or water *yagé*, to heighten his visions.

"He's a child of the jaguar," I said to Bailey, "and when he dies he will become a jaguar again and roam the forest." Bailey snorted and folded his arms across his chest. I noticed his face in profile, the nose projecting like a cleaver past the closely set eyes.

The *curandero* was arranging his paraphernalia on the table: transparent crystals, a fan made of leaves, necklaces of seeds and of jaguar teeth. A bottle of *yagé* stood to one side, its contents dark as if stained like the river by decomposing vegetation. Bailey and I handed over some crumpled bills. The deal consummated, we sat down cross-legged before the *curandero's* table. The earth felt cool and damp. Howler monkeys shouted nearby, and from deeper in the forest another troupe answered. Two squawking macaws dashed across the open space overhead appearing fuliginous against the evening sky. Encroaching shadows bled away the last of the light.

We had come to this remote region of South America seeking the rare blue orchid, *Aganisia cyanea*, not seen by botanists in nearly sixty years. Our investors hoped to clone the plant. If successful, Bailey and I, as chief scientists of the project, stood to make a fortune, and the present hardships would soon be forgotten.

The blue orchid was first collected in 1801 by Alexander von Humboldt and Aimé Bonpland along the Casiquiare, which connects the Río Negro in Brazil and the Orinoco in Venezuela at their headwaters. Richard Spruce in 1853 found a specimen growing near Manaus on the Brazilian Amazon; that same year he collected another on the upper Uaupés below the falls of Ipanuré. Afterwards, nothing until 1939, when a specimen was found at the headwaters of the Uaupés by José Cuatrecasas. Then in May 1942 Harvard ethnobotanist Richard Evans Schultes, having just recovered from a bout of malaria, stumbled across a blue orchid growing on a partly submerged tree trunk in the Río Karaparaná, Colombia. This was the last reported sighting. Comparing our quest with searching for a needle in a haystack would be an understatement. After three months of tracing Schultes' route through the Colombian rain forest, our prize seemed no closer than it had at the start.

The *curandero* was speaking softly in a monotone. The words were Spanish, either part of the ceremony prior to taking *yagé* or meant somehow as instructions. The few phrases I managed to hear lacked contextual meaning: *nadie puede comparársele* (no one can touch him), *un recién llegado* (a new arrival). I turned to Nai-kana and asked if he understood.

Nai-kana's eyes shone in the firelight like orbs of shiny obsidian. He seemed nervous or excited. No one could touch the jaguar, he interpreted. No one. Lately the water had begun to rise. The sound of its rushing would awaken the water boas, spirits who live as giant serpents at the bottom of the river. At the start of the annual flood the females come ashore, change into women, and capture husbands to take back with them. Boa women are enchantresses; no man can resist. If a boa woman appeared tonight the jaguar might protect us, provided the *curandero* had merged with the jaguar and not allowed its spirit to darken his soul from a distance. Tonight, Nai-kana said, would be especially dangerous. We had no choice but to participate in the ceremony. It was unavoidable. For emphasis, he slapped the ground beside him.

"What's he jabbering about?" Bailey asked. "Goddammit, I wish we had something to eat," he added bitterly.

Nai-kana glanced at me in alarm. Bailey's explosive anger could be disconcerting. "Hunger pangs," I said, rubbing my stomach. Nai-kana looked relieved. He understood hunger having lived with it all his life. True, our stores of food and medicine were exhausted, the result of being stranded upriver for nearly a month awaiting a supply plane that never came. There had been no choice but to push on. Starve here or starve downriver, what's the difference? That had been Bailey's attitude.

The *curandero* started to sing in an Indian dialect, slowly at first, and softly. Even in the absence of any wind, his voice was scarcely audible above the dripping of the forest. He spoke words that only Nai-kana understood. The *curandero's* wife built up the fire again before climbing the ladder and disappearing inside the hut.

Nai-kana leaned towards me. He explained that the *yagé* would cleanse us. Each of the *curandero's* objects contained meaning. One represented sounds made by the birds and other animals of the forest. Another allowed the *curandero*, when swept into his visions, to see deep inside our bodies. The wind and the fruits that fall from the sky were also set before him. After explaining this, Nai-kana became silent. I watched the *curandero*, contemplating his complete universe. Beside me, Bailey sighed.

The world, illusory though it is, can be fraught with danger. Fear accompanies every step: a viper dropping out of the canopy, a caiman sculling along the river's edge; in fever dreams malaria expels the soul. Everywhere, the inevitability of death and decay, the mineralization of leaves and flesh to their elemental constituents. The rain forest is a complex canvas, but the brush strokes are those of a minimalist. The *curandero's* chanting rose in opposition, forcing the untamed and dangerous to emerge from their hiding places and be swept away by his fan. He sang on, accompanied by the hissing of fan leaves pushing against tumid air. In the firelight I saw Bailey's jaw clenched tightly. He was eager to leave this place and move on. Time passes. More slowly for some than for others.

The singing rose again in pitch, now nearly falsetto. The *curandero* picked up a crystal and held it towards us in his open palm, moving his hand back and forth as if attempting to align it underneath a star. He repeated the gesture with another crystal, this time using his other hand. Then he picked up the fan and commenced singing. All around, toads and katydids began to trill.

The *curandero* uncorked the bottle of *yagé* and poured most of it into a wooden bowl. As the odor wafted to us, Bailey gave me an exaggerated look of disgust. The *curandero* dipped some up in a calabash and drank it down. The taste was evidently very foul because he immediately started to cough and gag. *Ayahuasca, ayahuasca*, he repeated, using the Quechua name for *yagé*. *Ayahuasca*. Vine of the soul. He looked at us, each in turn, his eyes even emptier than before. *Ayahuasca*. With great care he put on the necklaces. Nodding at Nai-kana, he refilled the calabash and handed it across the table. Nai-kana drank quickly, barely finishing before starting to cough.

I was next. I drank mine in a single swallow feeling my eyes water and my throat convulse as if touched suddenly by a bitter distillate of poison.

"Good stuff, eh?" Bailey asked. "What the hell, it can't be any worse than bad whiskey." He took his cup and tossed it off. "God, was I ever wrong!" he croaked. "Now what?"

"Now we wait," I said.

"For what?"

"Animal spirits." I turned to Nai-kana. *Ruda vitalidad*, I repeated. Nai-kana nodded solemnly.

"At least this vile shit ought to make us sleep," Bailey said. "I'm beyond being hungry."

The minutes passed, and the trilling of toads grew louder. I sensed the translucent fingers of unseen amphibians pawing at my ears, reaching in. A sudden warmth surged through me starting at the fingertips and moving swiftly into my torso. I turned slowly towards a different sound and saw Nai-kana puking. He grinned uncertainly and muttered, *Me asquea*. It makes me throw up.

Sí, I replied stupidly as I turned and threw up. I could hear the *curandero* retching in the bushes. He had managed to stand and move away from the fire. Beside me Bailey sat stoically with his long arms wrapped around his knees, but it was no use. There could be no holding himself together, and soon he too was retching. The vomiting came on suddenly and ended just as quickly. We lay prone beside the fire. I was drooling and felt the pungent earth against my cheek. Worms the size of large snakes crawled towards my open mouth seeking to merge its moisture with their glistening mucus. With a mighty effort I rolled onto my back.

Dentato, Nai-kana said. I looked to the side but saw nothing that was pronged. *Dentato,* he said again, immersed in a private vision, and then, *Me da vueltas la cabeza.* My head is spinning. I grunted, feeling guilty at becoming insensate.

Bailey was crawling in slow motion around the fire to the side nearest the river. He stopped partway to vomit. After finishing, he raised his head and looked through the flames at me, his blue eyes seeming to pierce my skull. *¡Azul!* I shouted, or thought I shouted. I looked again and the eyes had turned into blue orchids of the purist hue imaginable. *¡Azul!* I shouted again. The blueness burned into my brain, scorched the optic nerves, set the vitreous humor to boiling. Stars plummeted from the sky, exploding like Roman candles just overhead. I shut my eyes as protection against flying cinders, but the visions raged unabated. The thin veneer protecting the world I knew had splintered, and I was terrified, elated, charmed, paranoid.

¡Sapo! Nai-kana shouted. He pointed into the darkness. I concentrated, trying to see what he was seeing, and there it was, a man-sized toad walking upright, mimicking Nai-kana's bowlegged gait. *¡Ah, los colores claros!* Nai-kana exclaimed. I saw them too, cataracts of brilliant liquid dripping off the toad's head and oozing like molasses down its body. With each step the animal moved forward but came no closer.

There was a sound nearby, followed by a shower of sparks. A lithe figure backed swiftly away into the shadows. Goose pimples rose on my skin; I felt the urge to run and hide. I looked again. The *curandero's* wife was rebuilding the fire. I sighed. From his stool the *curandero* watched intently as if judging her.

Bailey still had not spoken. I looked through the flames and saw him squatting with one leg slightly behind the other, arms across his knees. His bush hat was tipped back and slightly askew and appeared to shift positions on its own. The soiled handkerchief tied around his neck struggled violently to unknot itself. He opened his mouth revealing a hole that grew wider until his face became a black ocean, his eyes hazy and indistinct as distant islands. The face returned, but only in outline, and from it came a protracted howl. I turned away, seeing a grinning skull wearing Bailey's hat.

The *curandero* sat on his stool staring in the direction of the river. I turned my head to look. Bailey was standing, arms hanging uselessly at his sides as if appended to someone else, the long legs wobbling as if made of rubber. Nai-kana shouted, *¡Cálmate! ¡Por allí a contraluz!* There! There! Over there against the light!

Then I saw it too. At the edge of the clearing directly behind Bailey a thick liana separated from the others and began to undulate, but the twisting flames obscured a clear view. The object inched closer, moving with the odd swaying motion of a serpent rising up to strike. Bailey was evidently unaware. I heard the *quok-quok-quok* of a night heron close by; a puff of air from a bat's wing brushed my face. The *curandero* began to chant and rattle his necklaces of jaguar teeth.

I looked at Bailey and saw a gigantic water boa appear at his side. Its skin—a mottled pattern of brown, cream, and black—glowed like satin in the firelight. Over time—I can't say how long—the boa turned into a woman of exquisite proportions, although the skin never changed. Nai-kana saw it too. This scaled creature wrapped its arms and legs around Bailey and drew him to the earth. He offered no resistance. Once prone, the boa woman changed again into a snake, enveloping Bailey in looping coils until only his hat and the soles of his boots were visible.

The *curandero* continued his chanting; Nai-kana and I simply stared. The creature's anterior end unwound from Bailey's neck and started to inch out of the clearing and down the slope dragging Bailey along.

The *curandero* rose and went through the purification ritual, first with Nai-kana and then with me. When he had finished it was nearly dawn. I fell into hallucinogenic sleep, drawn along by demons riding white horses. (Did you see the white horses, Nai-kana?)

When I awoke the fire was dead. Nai-kana slept restlessly

nearby; the *curandero* dozed with his head on the table. The air was cold, and mist had descended completely. The forest had stopped breathing; the day seemed stillborn.

I got up without disturbing my companions and walked down to the river looking for evidence of a struggle. Instead I saw two sets of footprints in the damp soil, one booted, the other bare and unquestionably human. Their outlines were distinct, indicating that Bailey had gone along without a struggle.

At the river's edge I came across a caricature of Bailey in the placement of his clothes. One soiled pants leg fell carelessly across the other; the arms of the shirt were skewed towards the embankment as if reaching for the worn boots. I thought of a collapsed marionette, or a war casualty, and clawed through the final curtain of undergrowth. Black water from the river licked at a floating sock, trying gently to swallow it. I picked up Bailey's folding hand lens, the kind we botanists use to examine the interior structures of flowers for the purpose of identifying them. Had he tried to use it in the dark?

Two sets of bare footprints led into the water. Just beyond floated the newly shed skin of a water boa. At that moment the sun broke through, and I saw that the skin lay in the shape of a human face. A partly submerged log formed the nose. Emergent sections of a moss-covered limb served as eyes, and in the middle of each was a plastic specimen bag. I waded out. On the labels were Bailey's initials and yesterday's date. Inside each bag was a blue orchid.

IT'S ONLY SUSHI

IN 1474, MAGISTRATES OF BÂLE SENTENCED A ROOSTER TO BE burned at the stake "for the heinous and unnatural crime of laying an egg." There you have it: a foul fowl, roasted alive (and probably unplucked) for laying an egg.

So said one of my many books stacked not very neatly over there against the cold wall. I'd like to believe everything I read, I really would. But if nothing about me in the morning paper is true, how can the rest be trusted, including the comics? A single bulb burns until lights-out, which leaves plenty of time. On overcast days the illumination is grainy and oblique.

Incarcerated because of an amphibian or a fish! At our second meeting I asked my lawyer, "Jesus, does seafood have rights?" He looked me over as if I might be crazy.

We shook hands. His was pudgy and well-nourished. His eyes were clear after years of reading only the labels on expensive bottles of wine; my own were bloodshot. "I found precedents in French law," I said.

He scraped back a chair and sat, letting his briefcase sag against the table leg like a tattered dog. To relieve the boredom he combed his hair. It was dark and glossy, the pelage of a flesh eater.

"In 1314 a bull in the village of Moisy escaped and killed a man. Officers of Charles, Count of Valois, imprisoned it. The bull was put on trial, convicted of murder, and hanged." No response. Probably my delivery.

43

"Hold the applause, there's more." I raised a finger, not lifting my eyes from the pocket notebook. This time I spoke louder. "In 1499, judges in the Cistercian Abbey of Beaupré condemned a bull to be 'executed until death inclusively' for having killed a boy of 14 or 15 years. And in 1697, a mare was burned at the stake by decree of the Parliament of Aix." I snapped the notebook shut and peeled off my glasses.

He leaned forward, his words sluicing out in garlicky stream. "You don't get it," he said. "This is murder, not some god-damn backyard barbecue, and this isn't France. It's not even Louisiana."

I countered by asking if his associates had looked for precedents in U.S. law.

He sat up and spread his arms. "Precedents for *what?* Drowning your wife and stuffing her in the freezer? Are you nuts?"

"No plea bargaining," I reminded him. "I'm innocent."

"Of killing your wife?"

"That wasn't my wife."

"So you say, but you killed *someone.*"

"Not necessarily."

He sighed and stood up clumsily, letting the briefcase flop onto its side. I waited for one end of it to bend around and lick the other, maybe between the brass latches.

That was then, this is now. Compared with my cell, the illumination here is much better. In my cell I was alone; here in the courtroom I have mannequins for company, some sitting silently, others rising occasionally to speak in gibberish.

"We could claim a religious exemption," I offer.

"Quiet," he says.

"Tell them I'm Muslim. The Koran makes all beasts and fowl accountable for injuries done to each other, but reserves their punishment for the afterlife."

"Will you shut the fuck up?"

"Listen, this is my *ante-*afterlife. You're supposed to defend me!"

"If you don't keep quiet there won't be anything to defend. Trust me."

Trust him? In what way? Admit to not knowing the consequences of my act, to being no more conscious than a falcon
snatching a pigeon? The insanity plea, I get it. Folks, this man
thinks computer games are real, that life as we live it—the
rest of us—is unreal. You kissed your husband goodbye at
the door? Dropped off the kids at school? Sat through a business lunch and got heartburn? Relax. None of it happened,
not really. Illusion. Waking dreams. Sleepwalking.

"Put me up there behind that railing," I whisper. "I'll set
everyone straight." I'm the only male present who isn't wearing a suit. The prison uniform is brown. Maybe this is only a
Kafka story and I'm a turd.

"Do you think I'm a turd?" I ask.

He turns. Little pockets of spittle form in the corners of his
mouth. "I think of you," he hisses, "as a suicidal moron."

I lean over and whisper ever so lowly, "The Prince of Darkness takes many forms. He can even be invisible (*aliquando
invisibiliter apparens*). He's particularly fond of inhabiting
swine, although in times of housing shortages not even blue-
bottle flies are chopped liver. Insects! Imagine that! Those
pointy little hooves . . ."

He grabs my hand and raises it slightly off the table, thinking perhaps it's a lever connected to my jaw muscles. My fingers are dry, his are wet and salty. He looks away from me,
across the room, and smiles lubriciously. The caring touch of
the counselor. Thank God his teeth have been bleached. Sta-
tistics prove that a white smile increases the chance of victory by . . .

The request was harmless, or had seemed so. She wanted
an aquarium, just a few fishes to give color and pattern to
the sunlight. A little aquarium, ten gallons, with stand and
filter and air pump, lid and overhead lamp. Why the lamp?
The sun doesn't shine at night, silly! She gave a *fin de siècle*
shrug with the sun at her back.

Theatrical in manner, nuanced of voice, somehow incom-
plete, like a sentence without a verb—I never knew when she
was acting. In self-defense, I came to treat every word or

action similarly. This naturally led to accusations of insensitivity, but what was the alternative? I had fallen in love with an actress, someone capable of expressing every emotion spontaneously.

Early in our relationship, in front of friends, she gave an alarming performance. Good-natured laughter shifted suddenly to heavy sobs with real tears. She ranted like a psychopath, glaring with wild eyes and pointing fingers at us. "I *am* a psychopath!" she shouted. "I'm a nightmare incarnate!" Partly to expiate our discomfort, we stood and clapped. She stopped and smiled acceptance, even taking a little bow, but it all seemed contrived. Who was she, really?

Understand this: my once-wife wasn't just a piecework woman, she was a piece of work. Artwork. Her life *was* her work, and she strode with fluid grace across its canvas. We hadn't any need of fancy objects; she took their places as living sculpture, posing beside the sofa or leaning like a ballerina to open a drawer. Music? Every sentence—each word—out of her mouth had been selected for the pitch and roll of its consonants, the fibrillated edge of its vowels, the slices of poetry that when strung together became an aria. Through a kind of levigation she separated any coarseness in herself and set it aside to rub against me, like sandpaper, until my psyche bled.

We were partying hard, seeing friends every weekend. One Saturday night the pack invaded. Our fishes were swimming gaily, wearing their dashing colors, when someone suggested swallowing them alive. We caught them using the little white net and washed them down with slugs of cognac until none remained. A lone tetra had tried to conceal itself behind the bubbling treasure chest, but we exposed it, pale with terror. I'm sure everything started that night.

The saltwater aquarium came next. The thing was enormous, taking up one end of the living room. We dumped in box after box of artificial sea salts, added tap water, and brewed up a small ocean. When the water cleared and the filters were humming and splashing, we went shopping for coral fishes. Everyone predicted they would die quickly, but they didn't. In fact, they thrived. Every Saturday morning I got out the bucket and siphon hose and cleaned everything—inside walls, decorations, gravel, filter—and replaced part of the water. It was a regular routine. I actually started to like it . . .

"Hey, don't space out. They can tell when a defendant is bored." He glances across the room as before and flashes the gleaming canines.

His opponent is droning away in front of us: ". . . DNA evidence obtained from the decedent, although very odd, clearly excludes from consideration . . ."

The human race. It excludes the human race from consideration. By then she wasn't acting; by then she had *become* a fish. Life imitating art right down to the scales and corpuscles. I lean over and whisper, "This is a clear case of speciation. Ask if they've tried matching her DNA with a flounder's."

"You're a sick sonofabitch. Don't say that stuff in my ear."

"Your ear is dirty. You ought to wash that ear, probably the other one too, and have the hairs trimmed."

This time he looks at me. "Fuck you," he says, a little too loudly. The group across the room glances up, but he reassures them with a smile.

". . . the body itself appeared to be mutilated almost beyond recognition. You, sir, as Chief Coroner, can you account for the unusual—I don't even know the correct descriptors . . ."

"The odd appendages and scaly-looking things? No, my office can't account for them. We sent tissue samples to the Armed Forces Institute of Pathology. No one there could identify them either. My report is in the record. I'd put my money on a perverted ritual of some kind, probably pagan . . ."

The table trembles. "Objection! Is my client on trial for what, in the Chief Coroner's opinion, might be his religious beliefs?"

"Sustained. Please strike the last sentence from the record."

I've considered this from every angle and dimension, replaying memories of her swaying in some invisible current, windows open, drapes blowing like kelp. The recollection makes me slightly seasick. To sit in a chair, she eased herself down by the "pectorals," meaning her arms, braking the descent gently. Instead of walking she glided, sometimes stopping to hover over a footstool or beside the refrigerator door. I still picture her shadow slipping warily through the foyer past lurking predators. She even bought new clothes, the better to blend cryptically with the kitchen linoleum.

I got used to this, but our friends never did. They stopped coming around. On weekends I pored over monographs on fish behavior, texts on the ecology of coral fishes, tomes on fish anatomy translated from German and Portuguese, while she paced in front of the aquarium attempting to school with its inmates.

"She ate only raw fish," I whisper.

"So what? I eat sushi myself," he whispers back.

"Her sushi was still flipping. She caught it with her mouth and swallowed it whole, headfirst."

He twists his shoulders away from me, hoping I'll disappear. The movement is barely perceptible, but the body language makes clear that a good client is silent.

The first to go was an emperor angelfish. I'd paid three hundred dollars for that fish! She and I together never spent half as much on dinner, even with wine. Expensive sushi, at a hundred dollars an inch. Suddenly she was standing on a chair with head and shoulders submerged in the aquarium, staring goggle-eyed at the terrified inhabitants. She wriggled the tip of her tongue like a frogfish wriggles the lure on top of its head. The effect was deadly. The emperor angelfish swam right into her mouth. Her head stayed under for ten minutes, maybe longer, and when she finally came up and turned to face me her lips were coated with fish slime.

That first incident led briefly to an amphibious existence when she seemed at home either inside the aquarium or out of it, provided the humidity of the room was near saturation. Being of slight build, she fit comfortably among the false corals and would lie on one side, watching me through the glass. I fed her live minnows.

"Your Honor, I have placed in evidence a deposition from the owner of a local bait shop. In it, he swears that the defendant purchased, over several months, thousands of saltwater minnows. Not once did he purchase any fishing tackle." My lawyer finishes by running his fingers through his hair.

"That's immaterial and irrelevant, your Honor."

"What's the point of this, counselor? I'm inclined to agree with the prosecution."

My lawyer stands up. His fingers are spread out on the table top. He's wearing a class ring on his pinky, but I can't read the name of the school no matter which way I twist my head.

"My point, your Honor? If my client didn't use those minnows to go fishing, what did he do with them? He fed them to his wife; or rather to that creature in the freezer that had *once been* his wife." He sits down and wipes his face with a white handkerchief. The monogram resembles a little gray moth pinned to one corner. "Jesus," he mutters.

Me? I lived on double-anchovy pizzas. Serve Mario down at the Leaning Tower with a *subpoena duces tecum*. Make him produce the receipts. But so what? It doesn't matter what I ate, what nutrients contributed to my dry epidermis and repaired any malfunctioning cells deep inside.

"I always wondered," I whisper, "is *subpoena* properly a verb or a noun?" There's no reply.

At first there was the problem of hypothermia, but her blood gradually turned cold. She came to feel like a fish, cool and slimy. Even her hair seemed to be matted with mucus. I gave the aquarium partial water changes every evening. By now she was its only inhabitant and placing a terrific strain on the filter. To increase her comfort, I had taken out the decorations. She didn't seem to mind lying on the gravel or sculling slowly in a circle.

I became concerned about her lack of exercise. One day I lowered the temperature of our hot tub and waited until the chlorine had dissipated. Mouthing the words *hold your breath* I pulled her out of the water and carried her outside. On seeing the hot tub she began to squirm frantically. I returned her to the aquarium and then dropped my slime-covered clothes into the washer. Between the minnow buckets and puddles of stale seawater, our house was starting to smell like a trawler.

The Chief Coroner is still on the witness stand. My lawyer rises.

"Did DNA from the decedent's body match that of the hairs obtained from her hairbrush?"

The Chief Coroner squirms. "Well, yes and no. We got partial matches."

"But wouldn't you expect a perfect match if the body in the freezer and my client's wife were the same, uh, person?"

"Yes, you'd expect that. However, in DNA analyses there's a certain degree of latitude that . . ."

"I see," my lawyer interrupts. "And were there signs of suffocation?" he asks.

"Do you mean, was there evidence of strangulation? None."

"I mean suffocation, not strangulation."

"The lungs—if they were lungs—were filled with salty water, probably from the aquarium. I think he drowned her by pushing her head underwater and holding it there." Then he adds, "In the aquarium."

"But suppose she breathed water, not air? What then? To kill her, did he hold her head *out* of the water? When a human drowns, the lungs ordinarily contain some water. If a fish had lungs, would holding it *out* of the water cause them to fill up with air? And wouldn't this be fatal?"

The Chief Coroner looks at the judge. "Answer the question," she says.

"I can't say. She had some weird structures along the sides of her neck. I've never seen anything like them. We called in an ichthyologist, but her results were also inconclusive."

"Were they gills?"

"Frankly, I couldn't tell you."

"Thank you," my lawyer says to the witness. To me he says, "I've eaten my last poached salmon, you bastard."

It was during a brown-out. I blame myself for not having a portable generator, but who thinks of every contingency? I was sitting in my chair reading Brian Curtis' *The Life Story of the Fish: His Morals and Manners*, when the lights flickered and went out. No more buzzing electrical appliances. My God!

No bubbling aquarium pump, no humming filter! The creature that had been my wife stirred off the bottom, raising a cloud of sediment. Her hands, now webbed, pressed against the glass. No ordinary fish, she sensed something was wrong.

I shoved a chair up to the front glass and began aerating with a bucket, scooping out water and letting it splash back onto the surface. It was no use. In that small volume the oxygen was soon depleted, and her panicked thrashing only hastened the end. She suffocated before my eyes, gasping mightily and arching her back. Damn Mario for delivering a pizza when I wasn't home and sticking it in the freezer.

That was then, this is now. "Ladies and gentlemen of the jury, have you reached a verdict?"

"We have, your Honor. We find the defendant . . ."

THE SELCHIE WOMAN

I HAVE NO MEMORY OF ARRIVING. NO VOICE OR SCENT, NO SENSATION of time having passed, connects me to this place. I simply came and stayed. Waiting. A day, a year, an eternity. Questions asked today are asked again tomorrow. Then and now are the same.

Lacking the capacity for sleep, I wander through dimensionless corridors looking for her, always seeking a clue. Days and nights converge in a sort of twilight. I don't know what the future holds—if indeed the future and past can even be distinguished. I travel but never arrive. The other inhabitants are no more knowledgeable than I. Like office commuters they come and go anonymously. Some leave and don't return, but others take their places.

When I was a boy my family took Sunday drives in the country. My sister and I sat on the back seat wearing dress-up clothes. I was too short to see anything through the passenger window except by looking obliquely upward. From this angle I could see only the tops of telephone poles linked by catenary wires. The wires rose abruptly to meet the next pole before descending again, on and on, forever it seemed, and I began to envision them as the troughs and peaks of ocean waves in a static sea. Occasionally there were birds. Starlings clinging to the swaying wires reminded me of gulls settling onto distant swells. I glimpsed these scenes momentarily from below, retaining an image of transparent water. Even childhood memories are about water, reminding me of her.

↫

"I hear he was a weird dude, a genius or something. Cigarette?"

"I'm trying to quit, but what the hell. After tonight . . ."

"How'd you do it, man? Nighttime. Tide coming in. Seems impossible to me."

"I just did it, I guess. It's not something you think about. I mean, you don't stand there in the surf wondering if you're going to drown."

"Yeah, I guess so. But my hat's off and all that. Are you warm enough, man? I got a blanket in my van. It's a little rank because of the dog, but it's wool. Want me to get it?"

"Naw. This one the paramedics gave me is fine. I'll stop shivering in a minute or two. It's more the excitement than the temperature. After all, this is summer, right?"

↫

"Sorry, I couldn't help overhearing your conversation with that older gentleman. Are you Scots?"

"Ay, Scots." She pulled out a chair and sat down heavily as the old often do after minimal labor.

"It's boring here, isn't it? Nothing ever happens."

"Borin', ye say? *Borin'*? No here, laddie! I'm up afore the sun, haulin' dross, lightin' ma fire, milkin' the coo. Ye cannae ken." She gave a derisive snort and began to fan herself with a newspaper.

To keep the conversation going, I asked, "The man you were talking to, is he also Scots?"

"Wha' mon?"

I raised my eyes to indicate the place where he stood, but he was no longer there.

"Are ye gaun tae hoome?"

"I don't know. I can't recall if I have a home."

"A body cannae sleep in the hedder. Follow me. I'll chum ye hoome." She got out of the chair and put a shawl over her head. The visible part of her face looked thin and sunken, the residue of starvation or sickness.

"There's a wee smirr," she remarked, adjusting the shawl. She craned her neck and looked up, as if inspecting the sky.

"Smirr? I don't feel any drizzle. It hasn't rained since I've been here."

"Then ye haena been tae Scotland afore. Come, we'll take a dauner tae yer hoose." She hobbled slowly away, back humped like a camel's. I started to follow, but just then she vanished.

I stopped and turned to go back, and saw a man looking at me. He was dressed in tweeds and high leather boots and carrying a walking stick. He said, "I maun hae scared ye comin' as I done oot o' the gloamin'."

"You didn't scare me," I replied. "Is everyone here Scots?"

"I see nae body but oursel'."

It was true. We seemed to be alone, although I could hear voices in the background, muddled and indistinct as if seeping through the walls of a distant room. They sounded calm, neither angry nor sad.

"Can you hear the voices?"

"I hear on'y the yammerin o' the wind. Some sae we're in fer a wee blaw, but I hae ma doots." He examined his pipe before knocking out the ashes on the heel of his boot. They fell glowing onto nothing.

"Yer claes are weet. Ye maun be freezin."

For the first time I examined myself. I was wearing a tee-shirt, cut-offs, sneakers without socks. Every part of me was wet, even my hair. What had happened?

"I'll take ye tae ma hoose. Ye cannae dry yoursel' oot here in the hedder and smirr." He turned and started walking.

I caught up with him. "What's your name?"

"MacFea. Ma hoose is ower yon brae. Ye can see the chimneys." I looked in the direction he pointed, seeing only what I always saw.

"Careful o' the bramble," he said without turning his head. He swung his walking stick as if knocking low branches aside.

We continued on. I glanced at my watch, which had filled with water but still worked. The sweep hand was moving counter-clockwise. Then I noticed that MacFae and I were

walking backward. My steps made a squelching sound. Mac-
Fae had been dry at first, but by the time we got to our destination the leggings of his pants were dripping and his boots
were dark with moisture.

"The muir is gey damp this day. I maun dress fer a funeral
in the village. Can ye hear the dirge?" He stopped all movement as if listening, then shook his head sadly and disappeared. I could still hear the voices.

I looked around but could not see any trappings of a
dwelling. There was no visible floor, no walls or ceiling. I lay
down where I stood and tried to sleep. Her image pushed
aside all other thoughts.

～

"He was a genius all right. He headed up the think tank
where I work. A real nerd, but a nice guy: honest, a hard
worker, but a sense of humor? Forget it. After he met her
things got worse.

"I remember working late one night, the whole group. Everyone was groggy from sitting around arguing and jotting equa-
tions on the chalkboard. One of the girls shot a spitball at
me. Imagine! A roomful of brain power, and somebody tosses
a spitball! Well, that woke us up. We had a good laugh, all but
him. Later he asked me what that thing was that Jeanie threw.

"We started having beach parties every Friday night. The
first ones were cold as hell. Even in April that wind coming
off the ocean can be awful. We came anyway lugging blan-
kets and food and booze. The menu changed weekly: Chinese one time, Mexican the next, and so on. Responsibility
for buying food and booze rotated. The duty roster was
posted on our internal e-mail. A party cost twenty bucks
apiece and the same for any guests. Our group works Mon-
day through Thursday, but sometimes we're there all night.
It's a good release from the tension."

"What did you mean by 'her'?"

"Oh, yeah. We arrived late one afternoon and set up. Some
of the guys collected driftwood for a fire, others carried
coolers from their cars. . . . In April the beach is deserted.

The air temperature was below freezing, the sea icy cold. And the wind! Everyone was wearing gloves and insulated parkas with hoods. As you know, the only available parking is that little lot across the road, and nobody pulled in while we were here. We'd have seen the headlights, and later when I talked to some of the others, no one recalled seeing anyone walking the beach with a flashlight. Even so, walking from where? To get to this beach your choices are to drive, hike all the way from town, or come by boat. Or swim.

"After we'd eaten he got up and walked down the beach a ways, out of the light of the bonfire, to take a piss. He was gone a long time, but no one really noticed. We were talking and drinking and snuggling up to keep warm.

"Suddenly he reappeared in the firelight holding hands with a girl. We all looked up in astonishment. There was instant silence. Before you ask why, I'll tell you. First, we couldn't envision *him* with a girl. Second, this was no ordinary girl, this was a *babe*, the kind you only see in photographs or the movies. She had long black hair that shone silvery in the moonlight, and she was wearing a thin short dress, a summer dress. No coat, no gloves. And she was barefoot. Her hair looked damp, like she'd been swimming, but who goes swimming around here in April? You wouldn't survive ten minutes.

"The girls in our group are mostly average looking. They have doctorates in math or physics, and primping takes a backseat to brains. These girls don't schedule makeovers from their office phones. If they telephone someone it's to check their data. Hell, one girl wears jeans every day of the year. Nobody's ever seen her legs.

"So, as I was saying, here stood the best-looking woman ever, and she's holding hands with probably the world's biggest nerd. Was I jealous? Damn right! She was all my fantasies in one package. You got another cigarette?"

"Sure. Take the pack. I've got another in my jacket pocket. Don't keep me hanging, man. So what happened next?"

"Finally Jeanie stood up and held out her hand. 'Hi,' she said. 'My name's Jeanie, what's yours?' Things started to get normal. The guys wiped the drool off their chins, and most of the girls were probably thinking, 'Who is this bitch?' but dealing with it. Jeanie stood there with her hand out, but the other girl didn't take it. Not from rudeness, I don't think. It was more like she didn't know what to do. He whispered something to her, and then she took Jeanie's hand and shook it up and down rather formally. Jeanie told me later that when she pulled her hand away it was wet.

"She said her name was Geira and she was from Scotland. We all relaxed after that. The Scots can be dour, and this girl was probably just shy. The two of them sat down outside our circle and talked only to each other. She never did put on a coat, and man, let me tell you, she didn't shiver either. Very strange."

〜

I drifted as if in a dream among islands of unconnected images. In the distance the same scene appeared: fishes and the sea floor as viewed beneath a filter through which only blue light could pass. The gloom was immense and pervasive. When I walked towards it, the scene receded in proportion with my every step. I tried running at it, but the distance remained constant. Schools of fishes came together seeking shelter in the rocks. They changed abruptly into flocks of birds gathering in a tree, then back into fishes. Bigger fishes—crepuscular predators—were emerging from the same rocks, their eyes carrying the glint of the hunter.

Here clocks reversed and reset themselves. Around me were wraiths in human form going about their business, some walking forward, others backward, never looking at each other. Which way did I walk? I could no longer be sure. Our collective locomotion seemed oscillatory, predictable, as if we were locked in a magnetic field, our movements regulated by an alternating electric current. We walked back and forth, advancing and retreating, some of us farther than others.

My thoughts began to clear, and I returned to images of Geira. We saw each other only on those Friday nights. No other time suited her. I never knew why. She came ashore in darkness, a lone seal humping up the slope of the beach dragging a large bag that she kept hidden somewhere under the sea. After sniffing my hands and ankles to confirm my identity, she rested briefly, maybe to gain courage.

The metamorphosis was sometimes too painful to watch, and at times I was compelled to look away. For long minutes she writhed in the sand emitting anguished wails. Then slits appeared in the silvery pelt. Indistinct at first, their edges widened and parted slowly like the covering of a ripe fruit. In actuality she was flaying herself, peeling away one skin to reveal another underneath. With every ripped adhesion her alienation from the sea grew stronger, her cries of pain more human. She emerged finally like an awakening chrysalis, damp and exhausted. Her feet were the last to pull free, then she was lying before me splendent and white in the moonlight, beautiful beyond belief. Of her former self, only her eyes remained unchanged.

After another brief rest she stood up, folded her skin into the bag, and put on a short dress made of lightweight material. I loved that dress, perhaps because it represented a sublimation, gracing the human part of her and offering hope of a lasting bond. I loved its lines and texture; I loved lifting the hem of it to caress her new thighs. I tasted her, sensed icy flesh tingle and start to glow, driven now by a human mind, a human heart, igniting my own flesh until we melted together in the overlapping flames. Each time we met I asked her to marry me and come live on the land. Each time she pressed a finger against my lips and looked at me through eyes like black pools. They held no expression. "I'll no awa tae bide awa," she whispered. I'll not leave forever. She said this, but as I was to learn, words have no meaning to a selchie woman.

"Hello, are you awake?" I sat up. A woman stood before me, features shaded by a shawl. She wore a long dress of indeterminate color. I couldn't tell whether she was young or old.

"Hello," I said back. "Have we met?"

"No, we haven't met, although I'm not surprised to see

you." She gathered the pleats of her dress together and sat down on a chair I hadn't noticed before.

"You aren't Scots."

"That's right. Why should I be? I'm Mr. MacFea's house-keeper. He's asked me to look in on you, see if there's anything you want."

"I could use something to eat. I can't remember when I last ate."

"We have no food. Your hunger will pass."

"I must ask you: Are we alive or dead? This seems like a nether world, Hell's waiting room. Is that an underwater view of the River Styx?" I pointed at the scene now becoming more familiar.

"What strange questions! Of course we're alive, why wouldn't we be? And if you're pointing at that painting on the wall, it was done by one of Mr. MacFea's cousins. The scene is a small island—actually a cluster of rocks—off the west coast of Shetland." She twisted her hands nervously one inside the other. I still had not seen her face, and when I made a point of looking directly at her, she lowered her head.

"Which island?" I asked, suddenly interested.

"Why, the Ve Skerries, about three miles west of a larger island called Papa Stour. The Ve Skerries are barren, inhabited only by seals and birds."

"I have a personal interest in these places," I said, "because I've come to find Geira. Do you know her?"

"Yes, I know her. Your task is impossible. Even if you find her, she won't remember you. Out on the Ve Skerries she's a selchie, not a selchie woman."

⤺

"Too weird! Want to go sit in my van where it's warm? I can start the engine."

"Thanks, but I feel fine. I'd rather stay here. Everyone's leaving."

"Tell me more about this guy, this genius. What's the story? He sure had something going for him."

"Can't tell you, don't know. She was strange, though, and her being around made him strange too. For example, they sat sipping Scotch at these parties, but it had to be Cutty Sark, nothing else. They'd look at the label and chuckle like it was a private joke. We never saw her except on Friday night, and she never arrived until after dark. How did she get here? Who knows? From what I can figure, she swam. They'd hang around a while, then go off down the beach. I swear, her hair was always wet.

"I couldn't bear the mystery. One night I followed them. It was clear, like tonight, with lots of moonlight. He sat down in the sand holding the bottle of whiskey in his lap. She opened this big bag she always carried and took out a fur coat. It was a *fur coat*, I swear! I was a bit loaded, but I know what I saw. She slipped it on and started to squirm around inside it. The coat slowly enveloped her until even her head and feet were covered in fur. By the time she'd stopped squirming the coat fit her like a glove—every curve and contour of her body.

"Then she got down on her stomach and started to move into the surf. She was literally humping along like a cater-pillar! Once in the water, she disappeared. I heard my girl-friend calling and had to get back.

"One Friday night in May she didn't show up. He got drunk and started raving about Geira, how he loved her and so forth, but that she was a 'selchie woman' and could never love him back. I didn't know what the hell he was talking about. 'She's a seal, what the Scots call a selchie,' he said. 'She can change back and forth between a woman and a seal. The night we met she'd just come ashore looking for a mate, and I happened to be standing there alone. She doesn't love me.' And he started to cry. The poor guy was devastated. I advised him to get professional help. The next week when she showed up everything seemed fine be-tween them."

"A seal? Jesus Christ! Too weird. Hey, want a nip? I've got a bottle of bourbon back in the van."

"Sure, why not. Might make things clearer."

"Yeah, what the fuck. Tomorrow's Saturday."

↬

As I was talking to the housekeeper, MacFea reappeared. He seemed nervous, almost distraught, and began pacing back and forth in front of me. I turned away in a final effort to locate the painting, and when I looked back we were alone, the housekeeper having disappeared. MacFea continued to pace, pulling on his long nose in agitation, one arm bent behind his back.

"Ye cannae gae tae her, laddie, she's a fey body, a selchie woman. She cast a cantrip ower ye so ye'd love her. Ay, she charmed ye. It's the way o' selchie women. Ye mean nae thin tae her noo. I saw her doon a' the firth, but she was swimmin' fer the skerries." He stopped as if trying to think of something else to say. Failing this, he struck a match against a wall I couldn't see and lit his pipe.

"I've got to talk to her," I pleaded. "I know this sounds trite, but I can't live without her."

"Ay, nor wi' her neither. Ye've go a sair hert, puir lad, but we cannae help ye here. Selchie fowk haena a memory such as other fowk; she disna want ye. If she lives, the bairn ye gave her will be born on the Ve Skerries, ha' selchie, ha' human, one day comin' amongst us like its midder." He shook his head sadly. "Ye're ha'way yoursel', ha'way tae yon."

"What do you mean I'm halfway? Halfway to where?"

"Tae ower yon." He raised a hand and pointed straight ahead, where I saw only the dim shapes of swimming fishes.

"You mean halfway into that sea?"

"Nae, laddie! Ha'way tae *yon*! Hae ye nae ees?" Then he was gone.

↬

"She was here tonight. I saw her."

"Where? With the bunch by the ambulance? I sure didn't see any gorgeous chick dressed in a fur coat. Pass over that bourbon."

"Sorry. No, I think I saw her out in the water, but events happened so fast I'm having trouble piecing everything together. The booze isn't helping. Maybe I didn't see any-thing."

"Tell me what you saw, man. This is interesting stuff, know what I mean? Weird, but interesting."

"Okay, for what it's worth I saw something surface out beyond the breakers. An animal of some kind, maybe a seal. Moonlight was glancing off the water, and suddenly a dark form popped up. And then the moonlight glinted off two reflective eyes. Just for a second, but long enough. Whatever it was ducked under. That's it. That's what I saw."

"Shit, man. Too weird."

⤚

"Mr. MacFea, please come back! I still need to ask you something! Are you there, Mr. MacFea?"

"Och! MacFea's here, laddie. Stop tha' haiverin' or ye'll wake e'en the dead. Wha' is it ye want?"

"What did you mean by 'if she lives'?"

MacFae was silent as if deciding whether to tell me.

Suddenly I knew. "Have the men from Papa Stour left for the Ve Skerries?"

MacFea reached into this vest pocket and withdrew a large gold watch on a chain. I leaned closer. The watch did not have a sweep hand, so I couldn't tell whether time was going forward or in reverse. MacFea himself might not have known.

"Accordin' tae ma watch, they leeft aboot seeven, but rowin' forward or backward I cannae sae."

"Are they going there to kill selchies?"

"Ay, the men need new rivlins made o' selchie sculp. When the auld ones leak it's like walkin' barfit. They trap the sel-chies ben a howe amongst the brae an' kill 'em wi' a dunt tae the heid. Then they sculp 'em soon efter so the stunned ones dinna slink away. The skerries rin wi' blood, and ye hear on'y the screamin' o' the kittiwakes and pickmaws an' the poundin' o' the sea." MacFea struck a match and ignited his pipe. I became enveloped in odorless smoke.

I scarcely dared to ask. "Will Geira be one of those killed and skinned?"

MacFea looked at me long and hard, his blue eyes seeming to sink deeper into his face. At last he said, "Ay, but a sculped selchie disna die ben the usual sense o' death . . ." He let the thought trail off as if reluctant to finish it.

The voices in my head ceased abruptly, their places taken by eerie moans like wind keening against rock. It was an anguished sound, neither human nor animal. I covered my ears, but it did no good. "What's making that sound?"

"It's the selchies on the Ve Skerries mournin' them who've lost their sculps an' are doomed tae live upo' the land fore'er. Wi'oot its sculp a selchie cannae enter the sea." MacFae shook his head. His life seemed filled with sadness.

"Has Geira been killed?"

MacFea's head didn't move. "Ay," he whispered.

There was nothing to say. I could hear an ambulance in the distance. The pitch of its siren deepened abruptly, an indication it had passed us and was moving away. I looked at MacFae. He was walking backward, and so was I. The ambulance was actually approaching.

Without warning MacFae's image flared before me, consumed in a white flame. Immediately the dim sea turned brilliant, its complement of fishes fading from view, the whole collapsing into a blinding white disk. I broke free of whatever forces shackled me to this place. Broke free and flew.

∽

"He's conscious. Hey, friend, what's happening?"

"I'm alive, huh?"

"You made it, but don't talk too much. I just pulled a trachea tube out of your throat. Had to start you breathing again. How'd you guys arrange to be drowning yourselves?"

"He followed his girlfriend into the surf and started to drown. I went to help him."

"We got you and him, but no girlfriend. She must have drowned."

"No, she probably swam away. She was a seal, a selchie woman. He couldn't let her go."

"A what? Too weird!"

"Haven't you and I just been talking on the beach? I recognize your voice. I'm sure we were talking."

"Not me, friend. I was giving you CPR and shouting questions and answers at my partner. You almost bought the farm. Your buddy didn't make it."

"He died? He really died?"

"Pronounced dead just a minute ago. I'm real sorry. There wasn't much we could do. When we finally got him to E. R. there was no pulse or heartbeat. We gave him closed-chest compression, but he didn't respond. He was holding onto a woman's dress. Too weird. Hey, here's my partner. Be patient. He's sometimes hard to understand."

"MacFea here, laddie. Sorry. We did aw we could. Ye might take this cutty sark. It'll be a comfort tae ye in his memory."

"I don't understand."

"The chemise. It's a wee bit soggy noo, but it'll dry oot fine. Made in Scotland, I'd sae."

"You called it a cutty sark?"

"Ay, in Scotland a sark is a chemise, and cutty means short. This one's a short chemise. A cutty sark."

GOODBYE, DOLLY

MRS. TOTIPOTENT, WIFE OF THE ESTEEMED RESEARCHER, KEPT sobbing into her fingers and repeating, "The poor lamb! The poor lamb!" But this wasn't what she meant, not exactly. Nobody cries because Dolly the sheep had been a clone.

We were sitting together in one of the booths outside the Lecture Hall. I was trying to comfort her, but my arm might as well have been a section of the padded railing, my sport jacket a strip of the dust ruffle. It was all very puzzling. I attributed her distress to a personal problem, certainly none of my business, and strained to hear the end of Dr. Morula's lecture.

"Embryonic clones are not the same as identical twins," he was saying. "Newspaper accounts are wrong in this respect. Except for *Doonesbury*, what's to be trusted in the media?" Sleepy laughter rose like a tattered moth to the lamp.

Dr. Morula let the interruption subside, then continued: "Twins result from *sexual* reproduction, each parent contributing fifty percent of the fertilized egg's genome. When the egg subsequently divides into two eggs—one representing each twin—the genomes are identical. Cloning, on the other hand, uses nuclear transfer technology, a form of *asexual* reproduction. A clone, unlike a twin, carries only the genome of the single donor, or 'parent.' Nothing except the nucleus is transferred to the recipient egg and, unlike twins, clones share nuclear DNA but not mitochondrial DNA . . ." He paused, I knew, to display another graphic on the overhead projector.

"It's so awful," said Mrs. Totipotent, at last abandoning the litany and raising her face out of my damp sleeve. Her salt-and-pepper hair was matted with perspiration.

"What is?" I asked, not realizing the premonitory nature of her remark.

"The professor and Synchrony! He's stolen her sample from the Tissue Bank and left me! Oh, the poor lamb!" Her feverish sobbing recommenced, still without revealing the lamb's identity.

I was vaguely aware of Dr. Morula's whiny voice, the Boston accent's glibness when confronted by certain consonants. "What made Dolly the sheep unique in the history of cloning?" he asked, hoping to defer narcolepsy among his listeners. "Simply that she was the first mammal cloned from a somatic cell of an *adult* donor, as opposed to an embryonic cell . . ." But I was no longer listening. Now I knew what Dr. Totipotent had meant by yearning "to be forever in Synch." He certainly had not meant his own research program in synchrony with mine or Morula's.

So! Their suspected affair had been real. Why was I surprised? Everyone at the Institute thought as much. I recalled having seen an unexplained damp spot on Totipotent's cloning counter, which I later caught him rubbing furiously with the sleeve of his lab coat. On another occasion I rounded a corner just as Synchrony emerged from the darkened Instrument Room. She glanced at me through steaming biohazard safety glasses while behind her Totipotent skulked among the Ohaus GA Series analytical balances. Yes, it suddenly came together.

Totipotent had been working in the field of transgenics, the transfer of genetic material between organisms of different species—in this case, mice and fishes. Synchrony Blair, his chestnut-haired assistant of muscular calf, had resigned more than a year ago to take a similar job in Oregon (according to Institute wits, a "missionary position"). Since her departure Totipotent had replaced her with a loyal girl fully at home in the Rodent Section. Still, he seemed despondent.

Shortly after Synchrony had cleared her desk of makeup and spike heels and turned in her photo I.D. badge, Totipotent ordered the lock changed on his laboratory door. This is standard procedure when personnel leave. Much of the Institute's work is funded by government grants requiring security clearance. We thought nothing of it at the time, although Totipotent became increasingly secretive, keeping his door locked even during working hours and prohibiting everyone, including his own staff, from the Aquarium Room. Morula and the rest of us had no idea what he was up to, assuming it was some top-secret project. Not even the Institute's Interim Director seemed to know, and there the matter rested for months. A scientist doesn't enter another's lab unless invited, and we never were.

Totipotent spent hours at a time in the Aquarium Room. We knew this because his shoes squelched when he appeared at coffee breaks. He caught colds frequently, as people do when their feet are constantly wet, and sat silently among us sniffling and wiping his considerable nostrils on the sleeves of his lab coat. He became morose, visibly smaller and hunched, behaving like someone who has lost his *élan vital* and is now bereft of ambition. How wrong we were! Soon the terrible secret would be known.

In late autumn Totipotent became his old self again: truculent, contumacious, possessed of protean knowledge. He strutted confidently, pipestem clenched between yellowed teeth, patches of hair bristling like islands of forb on a barren mountain.

"They're breeding at last!" he shouted one morning at coffee break. Outside, sleet hammered the windows and naked trees writhed like hydras. "We have several clutches of viable eggs!" He was referring to his beloved wolffish (*Anarchichas lupus*), a surly species of sinuous form growing to nearly two meters in length. Its upper and lower jaws contain thick protruding canines backed by multiple series of crushing molars. "It won't take long now," he added cryptically.

After Totipotent recovered from his mysterious malaise, he and Synchrony ceased to be objects of conversation. Around the Institute, memories of their antics dimmed with winter's pale sun; gossip that had entertained us previously was pushed aside by the realities of teaching, research, budgets, and grant proposals. No one noticed when Totipotent, in the manner of a hibernating vole, disappeared completely into his laboratory and adjoining Aquarium Room. It was during this period that his wife found me sitting outside the Lecture Hall and unburdened herself. If only I had listened carefully, shown more sympathy . . .

Just as we became aware of his absence, Totipotent emerged once again. It was shortly before the winter holidays. Snow lay everywhere and the Institute's grounds resembled a New England Christmas card. In the intervening weeks the pile of mail in his office had finally, of its own mass, toppled onto the floor, forming a scree against his desk, but within days all clutter disappeared. We learned later that he had simply thrown everything away unopened.

"Well, old boy!" Totipotent exclaimed one afternoon in the hall. "How goes the war?" His face had a look that simultaneously arouses loathing and pity. He meant, of course, my research and success in securing grants, but the words sounded specious. Had he attended staff meetings or even appeared occasionally at coffee breaks the question would have been superfluous. I mumbled something pleasant and unconsciously stepped back, the better to see his face in the dim light. He looked pale, almost jaundiced, and undeniably older, resembling someone who has survived a life-threatening illness or frightening psychological trauma.

"Seen the staff photo?" he asked loudly. I had, of course.

"Yes," I replied, then to smooth over a certain uneasiness, added, "but I don't photograph well."

Totipotent clapped a hand on my shoulder as he might a pimply undergraduate's and explained in a stentorian voice why, after a lifetime of seeing our own images reversed in mirrors, a photograph depicting our true orientation somehow doesn't look right. "Your feelings on the subject are perfectly normal," he said with assurance. It was vintage Totipotency, first embarrassing you with his superior knowledge, then offering a lame gesture of restitution.

Totipotent was undeniably an intellectual, one who squirrels away ideas and facts as others collect fairy rings, netsukes, or old fado albums. At the Institute's Christmas party the previous year someone had drunkenly remarked how nature abhors a straight line. "Not so!" Totipotent had cried, jabbing his index finger at the ceiling. "There are crystal facets, aquiline noses, cleaved graphite, the edges of sweetgum leaves, wings of a tropicbird, a box crab's carapace, and the boles of totara trees as viewed in the vertical plane!" He then paused thoughtfully. "I could come up with other examples, given time, but you see my point." And he reminded his puzzled colleagues to read Borges, who suggested that copulation and mirrors are abominable because both multiply humankind.

To Totipotent, a native of British Columbia, childhood memories were scenes projected onto a dripping landscape, whispers born of a solitude shaped by shaggy forests, the call of the owl. We were never close, he and I. His strut, as I discerned eventually, was not an affectation of arrogance but as much a part of him as the chicken walk is to a chicken, a simple genetic trait behaviorally expressed.

At our most recent Christmas party Totipotent approached a group of us chatting quietly and interrupted the Interim Director in mid-sentence. "I quote Enzo Ferrari, the carmaker!" he yelled, as if trying to be heard in a noisy room. "'A car is a rather beautiful and fascinating thing. It is because of that, and because there is no perfection but only evolution, that I continue to dream.'" His wife started to cry, which the rest of us attributed to excessive drinking. Totipotent winked knowingly, bushy eyebrows rearing like opposing mice, and left us to reconcile the deterministic bent of automobile design with natural selection's stochasticism.

Totipotent had been a student of Wang Sun Yap who, in the nineteen-seventies, had successfully cloned frogs and several other ectotherms—notably the wolffish—using skin cells taken from adults of their own species. No sooner had Totipotent established residence at the Institute than he requested an Aquarium Room to continue and advance the work of his mentor. Within months it was under construction, and Totipotent's career sailed ahead. Later we wondered if he had ever considered the consequences of matching two such disparate species, one a nonthinking predator, the other the evolutionary zenith of thoughtful predation. His laboratory notebook, as we learned in the end, told a story of genes that until his meddling had never met but merely hailed each other like distant trains across a vast prairie. Perhaps by then Totipotent's fate had been decided and he was a white-coated Kurtz shuffling without integrity or remorse into his private heart of darkness.

I shall call you Melusine, reads a late entry in his lab notebook. The phrasing and formality have an Old Testament quality, as if Totipotent saw in himself elements of the Creator. Elsewhere he muses lightly, *Is there sex after death? Yes, my Melusine. For us, always. But I must leave you alone now in your dish and go pipette some fluids. . . .* Clearly, he was making these entries while the creature was simply a cluster of nonspecialized cells, visible only to his imagination!

How many failures had there been before success? The entries go on for pages: hundreds, maybe a thousand failures before those few cells gained strength and proliferated, becoming the monster he called Melusine. Noting that early forms of life undoubtedly appeared on Earth countless times before a few cells survived, he writes: *How frustrating for God to watch life slip through his fingers! What infinite patience! But my patience is infinite too, and my Eve will be even more lovely than His.*

The final entries are written in an angry scrawl; paranoia jumps off the page: *Those bastards! The prevarication, their snotty attempts at social superiority!* He then adds poignantly, *I have you now where we can never be separated.* In Totipotent's disintegrating mind Melusine had become Synchrony, no longer beyond his reach but confined and accessible within glass aquarium walls, available to him always.

Totipotent's achievement was indeed remarkable. The notebook describes how a nucleus taken from a single cell of Synchrony's tissue was introduced into the developing egg of a wolffish. Initial failures caused by differences in temperature requirements of the respective cellular constituents were surmounted by using certain cryoproteins. But these details of the specialist are not of concern here.

After the Christmas holidays Totipotent once again dropped from sight, his presence known only by the wedge of light that crept from underneath his door and sometimes a faint odor of canned *vol-au-vent relleno de raviolis* warming in the microwave. By early spring he was nearly forgotten. Then on a morning in March the alarm sounded indicating a major seawater spill.

I rushed to the Aquarium Room, the Interim Director and Morula close on my heels. Totipotent's CD player had evidently been resetting itself, and Wagner's *Wahlspruch für die deutsche Feuerwehr* ended just as we broke open the door, the final notes fading seamlessly into white pump noise. Metallic echoes of rushing seawater ricocheted from the walls.

Totipotent, grotesque in death, was blocking the spillway of the main experimental aquarium causing influent seawater to overflow onto the floor. The high water level had pushed up the float of the float valve and activated the alarm, a standard safety precaution to prevent flooding nearby laboratories. Totipotent's lab coat was unbuttoned, undulating slowly like waving kelp; his penny loafers glowed greenly from algal accretions. He had probably been dead a day or two before bobbing up against the spillway grate, immediate decay retarded by the frigid water. Mrs. Totipotent's "poor lamb" could be none other than the unfortunate professor himself. She had known about his work all along.

As we stood speechless, Totipotent tumbled over as if caught in a sudden undertow. His corpse submerged briefly before the shoulders turned towards us. We gazed in horror at his head, which had been crushed between powerful jaws like the shell of a whelk. Under and around Totipotent's body flashed Melusine, mouth opening and closing rhythmically. Her eyes were wide and expressionless as a wolffish's, the bare breasts hard and scaled. As we approached, arms opened as if welcoming us; fingers curled in unison, beckoning us on, although the creature's expression never changed. Long strands of chestnut hair trailed upward, collapsing and expanding in the currents like the bell of a medusa.

All at once Melusine dashed to the surface, causing a wave of cold seawater to surge over us. In the confusion she grabbed Morula by the collar and lifted him off his feet. Had it not been for the Interim Director and me holding onto his legs, the poor man would have been pulled into the aquarium, Melusine's next victim. In the end we were a match for her: she ripped away Morula's coat and shirt, we were left holding his shoes and trousers, and Morula himself lay gasping between us dressed only in brown Argyles and boxers decorated with grinning mermaids.

Shivering, we retreated to a far corner of the Aquarium Room and discussed strategy. Was she capable of reproducing? She was, of course, but we had not yet discovered Totipotent's notebook. The Interim Director reminded us of potentially disastrous publicity if word of Totipotent's creation were to reach the newspapers. "So long, Institute," he said sonorously. "Goodbye to your careers. Future National Science Foundation grants? Ha!" He drew the edge of his hand across his throat.

We discussed killing the creature by introducing rotenone into her aquarium water, but such talk was quickly set aside: we were bound by the Hippocratic oath. Carefully lifting the spillway grate with a broom handle, we watched Melusine slither into the outflow sump and from there to the sea. My God, I thought, as her tail slipped from view, what have we done?

HOME IS THE SAILOR, UNDER THE SEA

HE WAS A SAILOR RETIRED FROM THE SEA, BUT NOT ITS RHYTHMIC heaving, the circadian pulse of its tides. Objects washed up in the night collected at his doorstep like disassembled memories. In the fragments of shells and bits of seaweed lurked a damp emptiness similar to his own. Their immobility mocked him; their silence reminded him of his own death, so that he was forced to look away.

His personal history had vanished into a dry haze. Darkness became intolerable. He slept in fitful disharmony, stepping easily into his dream until sleep and wakefulness were the same. Hiiaka always appeared, her black hair sliding away into indigo. Countless times he reached over the side, grasping nothing. Frantic, he jumped overboard, pulling hand over hand down shafts of moonlight, through tremulous bubbles that wobbled out of the abyss. He touched one just as a cloud obscured the moon. The handholds dissolved; he floated up, feeling the sea's lessening weight on his lungs. Upon regaining the air, imploding echoes of failure and loss passed through his lips, and he awoke with a howl, skin tingling as if abraded against the darkness.

At other times the sounds and images—even the sight of his own hands—assumed dreamlike qualities. Put away after one dream, the bent fingers unfolded like stiff flowers in the next, and on through an endless sequence of wakefulness masquerading as sleep. He watched as his hands, without any apparent instructions, baited hooks, opened coconuts, pounded breadfruit pulp. If he muttered surprise, the other villagers laughed and shook their heads.

Once in the thin darkness before dawn his mind suddenly cleared. The dream had released him. Overhead a gray lizard stalked a moth along the roof supports. Awareness and recognition fused once again; here was correlation of life with movement. He turned sideways. Pale light seeping through holes in the thatch settled on the hut's sandy floor, cratering his footprints in shadow. Silhouettes of palms creaking and shivering in the doorway sprang pertinaciously from memory, their shapes at once familiar. The land odors were sharp, as if he had been away at sea; they told him it was late spring. He must act quickly before the haze returned.

Outside, objects of daily use seemed clean and bright, as if freshly washed. He glanced around trying to recall their histories. Did they belong to him or to others? What others? Indistinct images of relatives and friends came to mind, but time had passed. Their faces seemed young, too young. Perhaps they had moved to other islands; maybe they were dead.

He walked to the beach where his canoe lay tethered like a beached turtle. Its stern held a silver pool of rainwater. In its surface he saw a wrinkled face with rheumy eyes, framed by long white hair. The eyes smarted, releasing unsuspected feelings. He knuckled them roughly, but the image hung pale and ghostly behind his eyelids as if frozen in a lightning flash. The years had left without him, like birds lifting into the wind.

Behind his hut, in a clearing filled with sunlight, he built a drying rack on which he laid slices of banana and coconut. The giant breadfruit tree nearby was heavy with fruit oozing white sap. He picked several fruits and baked them in his earthen oven, afterwards removing skin and seeds and pounding the pulp with a club dipped frequently in water. The doughy pulp was laid in sheets across the rack to dry. He discovered several sweet potatoes cached in the cool ground underneath the hut. He baked them, sliced most of them, and set the slices on the rack.

Voices drifted from the village, but he had no wish to visit.

He could smell cooking fires and hear children laughing. Constructing the drying rack and preparing the fruits and vegetables had taken all day. In the failing light he crafted fishing lures from pieces of turtle shell. When it became too dark to see, he ate a cold sweet potato and went to sleep.

He awoke again before dawn. From coconut husks scattered on the ground he pulled fibers and twisted them into string by rolling them against his thigh. The finished strings he spliced end to end and braided into a rope that he soaked in the sea to toughen. Other coconut fibers were dipped in breadfruit sap and pounded into cracks in the hull of the canoe. He leveled the canoe and filled the hull with seawater so the wood would swell, pressing the edges of the cracks against the new fibers and forming a tight seal. When night came he began weaving a sail from pandanus leaves, relying in the absence of light on knowledge stored in his fingers.

After three days he bailed out the canoe, attached the sail to the mast, retied the outrigger using his new rope, and put to sea. The hull did not leak, and the new sail, stiff and dry, crackled and chattered. He tightened the lines, tacking back and forth across the wind, laughing and wiping spray from his face. After catching several *máhimáhi* by trolling with his lures, he returned to the beach. He cut the fish into thin slices that he soaked in seawater before smearing them with their own blood and spreading them on the drying rack.

In the afternoon he collected other provisions: coconuts both green and ripe, lengths of fishing twine, and empty coconuts in which to store water. These last he filled through their open eyes and sealed shut with coconut fiber dipped in breadfruit sap. Two would be needed for each day at sea unless there was rain.

He was conscious now that his back hurt. Squatting for long periods numbed his legs. When kneeling before the earthen oven, his knees seemed filled with the spines of sea urchins. He remembered none of this pain from before. Perhaps it was better to live thoughtlessly, confined like a beast within a pen of dreams.

The oven needed fuel. Grunting, cradling an armload of

driftwood, he gauged the distance back to the hut . . . too far; the load was too big. With another grunt he dropped everything, assembled a more modest burden, and trudged on through the sand. Yes, he decided, pain was preferable to not feeling. Before, each day had rolled under him like a sea swell, rising and falling yet staying in place while the sea's energy rushed past. His life had risen and fallen with the days, leaving him soaked and dying, no closer to Hiiaka. Now he could go; the knowledge was still there. As a young man they had called him *ho'okele,* or sailing master.

There were certain protocols, although he no longer cared. The *kilo hoku* from the village might consent to bless his trip, but at the cost of considerable distraction. Other villagers would question his motive or sanity; even worse, someone might ask to come along. He could have baked a pig if he owned one, or chewed and mixed *'awa,* but so little time remained. At any moment the haze could return. So he scanned the sea and sky for signs of bad weather, seeing no unusual wave formations or broken clouds rushing before a storm. The sea was nearly flat, and the only clouds were *newe-newe,* puffy on top with their yellow bellies pressed against the horizon.

His course would be south and slightly east; the altitude of the fixed star *Hokupa'a,* from where he stood, was two fists above the horizon. As he crossed the invisible boundary separating the northern and southern worlds, *Hokupa'a* would lie directly on top of the sea. He had made this trip several times, but always in a large double-hulled canoe with many others. The journey had taken thirty to forty days in each direction, depending on winds and currents. When he left he would be sailing against both.

Two weeks passed, and everything was ready. In his last dawn ashore he loaded the canoe, covering the provisions with a tightly-woven mat of pandanus leaves to protect against sun and sea spray. Food and water were sufficient for a month, and he would trail lures hoping for fresh fish. Nights would be cold and often wet, the days blistering unless there was cloud cover. Comfort mattered little. He thought instead about Hiiaka, who used to shiver when the sun rested even briefly behind clouds. If raindrops or a cool breeze touched her skin in the night she moved closer, absorbing his warmth. Before sleep she often rubbed her arms and legs with crushed *pikake* blossoms. The scent rose between them, mingling with their heat like smoke from a hidden fire. He smelled it now, as he had that morning upon awakening to see the lizard watching him.

Overnight an offshore wind had flattened the sea and bunched its surface into glittering bands made orange by the sun. Gulls lifted from the beach as he walked, appearing black and shapeless against the eastern sky. He untied the canoe and pushed its bow into the low surf. Sand and broken shells shifted under his feet, solid and reassuring. From the land itself he had taken only a large stone, little different from the other, that first stone. Without looking back, he climbed aboard and paddled until clear of the breakers, then raised the sail.

By afternoon his island had disappeared, although signs of its presence remained: drifting vegetation, a reef of high clouds, the swells pushing outward around invisible headlands. At evening, flocks of *noio* heading back to shore after a day of fishing revealed how far he had traveled. At sunset he caught a *káwakáwa* that he sliced into strips and ate raw with pieces of dried banana and breadfruit and washed down with a coconut shell of water.

In the darkness he held position by keeping *Hokupa'a* behind him, tacking off course alternately to the southeast and southwest, but plunging ever southward. On each tack he napped, feeling in the sea's motion any deviation from the course. His body fell easily into the jostling of the swells, and he imagined himself cradled between the gigantic breasts of a sea goddess. Dozing, rousing himself in half-sleep to alter course slightly, he pressed a hand to his chest. Soon he would put his ear to Hiiaka's as she slept, hearing behind her flesh and ribs the echoes of his own heart.

In the morning a flock of *manu-a-ku* passed overhead, sunlight glancing off their white plumage. They dipped and swirled. He watched, estimating the distance he had traveled. Like the *noio*, the *manu-a-ku* return to land each evening, but the *manu-a-ku* travel three times farther out to sea. If the wind held he would not be seeing them tomorrow.

After tying off the lines he baited two lures with strips of skin from the *káwakáwa* caught the previous day and trailed them off the stern within easy reach. The morning sky portended no rain. For breakfast he ate dried banana and coconut and drank a coconut shell of water. He thought about saving the empty vessel to fill with future rainwater, but instead watched it bob away among the fluid blue hills. He stood and urinated over the side, thinking of the wasted water in his stream. The *manu-a-ku* did not need fresh water, nor did the fishes beneath him; only humans needed it. Eventually he would sink like a fish into the sea's dim chasms, hearing no sound, seeing no sun. From down there the splash of a man's urine must sound like rain falling on a roof, insignificant as raindrops.

There was nothing to do except maintain course and check the baits. During the day he marked his course by the sun. At night the stars rose at known locations on the eastern horizon and set at known places in the west. As a young man he had been taught to use a star compass with sixteen points around the horizon. Each point represented the middle of a house of the same name. East is *hikina*, or "arriving," where the sun and other stars arrive on the horizon. West is *komohana*, or "entering," where the sun and other stars enter the horizon. North is *'akau*, south is *hema*. . . . He knew the rising and setting places of the stars in the different houses of the sky. As he traveled south and crossed the line that separates north from south, the rising and setting points of the stars would shift southward, and the farther south he sailed the greater the shift would become. The moon rises and sets every night in a different place, but with knowledge a sailing master could also use the moon to hold course. He knew these things. They were no less familiar than his thumbnails, yellowed and ridged as the backs of old seashells.

In the beginning there had been no light, only darkness.

The progenitors—Rangi our father, Papa our mother—lay together inseparable, Heaven and Earth. Their six sons grew tired of eternal darkness and discussed whether to kill their parents, but one brother, Tane-mahuta, father of the forests and all that inhabit them, lobbied to pry them apart. At last, five of the six agreed with this plan, and one by one they tried, but their parents were too vast. Then it was Tane-mahuta's turn, and with a mighty effort he separated Rangi and Papa. At that moment numerous human beings became visible, having been concealed until then.

But Tawhiri-ma-tea, father of winds and storms, had never agreed to the plan, fearing his kingdom would be destroyed and the world would become sunny and beautiful. Instead, he rose Heavenward with Rangi, his father, becoming lost in the anonymity of stars. There Tawhiri-ma-tea produced many offspring, including those he sent to the north, east, south, and west, giving them the names of those winds, but keeping for himself the mightiest of winds, the hurricane.

The progeny of Tawhiri-ma-tea lurk in rain squalls, waterspouts, clouds of all colors and shapes, thunderstorms. Before Tawhiri-ma-tea's fury even Tangaroa, father of the oceans and all that live in them, hides in the deep for safety. These and similar conflicts became the way of the world, and so it has been ever since. Despite everything, Heaven and Earth are still in love. When Papa sighs, the mist rising towards Heaven is her bosom; and as Rangi bemoans the loss of his wife, the tears he lets fall from his eyes we call the dew.

Can you hear their voices? I hear murmurs, whispers, muffled weeping. I remember from the time before the haze, the time of memory. I must turn away, ignore them, the parents of my race. Have I too become a god? A voice hasn't any weight or substance; it leaves no imprint, no sign of its passing. Voices falter on air; the wind erases them. They were never here.

Under me are drowned women, half fish now. I know; I've seen them. One surfaced many years ago while my companions slept. Our canoe was becalmed, and I stood alone under the jabbering sail. She stuck her head up and looked directly at me, eyes reflective and hopeless as those of a fish, her mocking smile evoking in me a deep sorrow. Is that all? I thought. If I tumble overboard and drown, will my legs fuse at the knee and ankle? Will my feet curve back, becoming a crescent like the tail of an *ahi*? And which will I be upon arriving at that endless banquet under the sea, pursuer or pursued? Then she was gone, leaving a black circle in the moonlight. At dawn, while the sailing master was taking his morning piss, I described what I had seen. It was a woman's ghost, he replied, not a real woman. Perhaps a woman long since drowned, perhaps not. Who can tell? But I know what I saw; a ghost casts no shadow. There I go again, talking to myself . . .

Is it true? Are there lands elsewhere that are dry as dust, hot as an oven of stones in the ground? Are there places where men have never glimpsed the sea? Some say that across the world are islands so vast a war canoe sailing before the wind cannot pass around them, not even in a thousand days and nights. Such a thing, of course, is preposterous.

You are old and weak! screams the south wind. Little devils sent by Tawhiri-ma-tea, they're sneaking up from the port side along our western tack. Be careful, Hiiaka! Don't stand up, you might fall overboard! The wind strengthens; cold spray climbs over the gunnels and hurls itself against my skin like a shower of stones. Hiiaka was there once, in my line of vision, hair flying outward between the mast and wind-driven sea. Her feet, unknown to me, rested on a stone that no one saw. Tangaroa dives under the keel and hides, the coward! Afraid of his own brother! I can't protect the gods from each other. . . . And when I look up, she's gone.

He was suddenly aware of his finger coming into focus. Pointing. Admonishing the unseen. A remnant of something said became the shriek of a tern. So that's how it was: he shouted, birds replied. The haze had returned without warning, attacking silently like *niuhi*, the maneater, who leaves behind only dismembered scraps unfit except for scavengers. The mind stretches, extending distances between past and present before contracting and reassembling itself in a different form. Soon his two halves would pull apart like old rope, trailing the frayed ends of memory and recognition. Then he would be like the birds and fishes, able to find his way and feed himself, but no longer a child of the Ancestors.

How long had his mind been away? It was daylight, but which day? After securing the sail, he lifted the mat and took inventory of his stores. Since the last time he could remember he had eaten food for three days and drunk six coconuts shells of water. The stone remained in place, dense and implacable. So . . . three days of bellowing at terns, of raging against *malolo* the flying fish. What a fool he was! He inspected the vessel, making minor repairs and adjustments and at sunset tacked southeast. The taller seas were now against his starboard bow. Soon *Hokupa'a* appeared over his left shoulder. He ate some dried fish and celebrated his mind's return by opening a green coconut.

The lures had not fished well in his absence, and he scolded himself. The bone hook was missing from one; the thin strip of fish skin dangling from the other was now several days old. No sensible fish would be interested. He tore it off and threw it away. After repairing the broken lure, he decided to keep both aboard for the night to let them rest. Rejuvenated, they would fish better at dawn.

He continued on the southeastern tack until the moon began to wane, then came about and headed southwest once again. In the night he started to shiver, but warmed quickly after eating some dried breadfruit. Even though he lived closer to the sea than to the clouds, he was more like a bird than a fish. The blood of a bird when you kill it is warm. Its heart pumps like a human heart. A fish's blood is always cold. Did fishes have hearts? Probably not, he thought, because then their blood would be warm too. The heart is the body's sun, and when the sun in the sky sets, the blood is soon cooled despite efforts of that lesser sun beneath the ribs.

Against the pale streaks before sunrise he saw the stars *Ke Ali'i o Kona i ka Lewa* and *Puana-kau* set together. He was not quite halfway to the imaginary line separating the northern and southern worlds. When clouds later obscured the sky, he held course by feeling the motion under him, knowing that ocean swells move directly from one house on the star compass towards another of the same name in the opposite quadrant.

The next day his lures caught three *opelu palahu*, which he ate raw with slices of dried sweet potato. The fresh food warmed his stomach. By mid-morning the warmth had spread to his back and knees. He felt young and supple. Hiiaka reminded him to keep his lures in the sea. Dried food will not sustain you, she admonished him. Soon you and your food will look alike, wrinkled and unappealing. And then what? I'll tell you. No decent woman will have you, including me. He imagined the giggles that followed, the hand pressed to his cheek. Ha! he thought. She's right. He dutifully baited his lures with the shiny skin and entrails of the *opelu palahu* and tossed them into his wake.

The swells had grown. Dark clouds—*'ilio uli*—rose in the distance as if peering at him over the edge of the world. By afternoon, legs had descended from their bellies, and they danced in a ragged line across the sky. He was reminded of the great battle once fought on his island between the gods. Tawhiri-ma-tea, appearing as a hurricane and driving rain before him, attacked Tane-mahuta, god of the forests and all things made of wood. Great palms and breadfruit trees were ripped from the earth and hurled at one another; canoes were dashed against shoals of coral. Many people died, some crushed like insects as they fled into the writhing forest. Ever after, Hiiaka trembled at the sound of thunder and ran to him for protection, hiding like a child against his chest.

Tawhiri-ma-tea came in the night. Putting his lips to the mast, he moaned loudly. Tawhiri-ma-tea grabbed the sail at its edges and shook until it rattled and fought wildly against the lines. All around was blackness, like the dark that covered the world before Rangi and Papa were separated and light could fill the space between them. The sea spray felt unusually cold. He needed food, but the mat covering his stores was secured tightly.

Just as he untied it the sail line slipped through his other hand, causing the canoe to lurch suddenly and lose its heading. With its outrigger momentarily submerged, the hull corkscrewed, backing its stern into the swells and letting in the sea. He dropped the lines for fear the sail would rip away and began bailing with his hands, but for every handful thrown overboard, two more took its place.

Tawhiri-ma-tea's voice had risen to a shriek, and the spray was now mixed with rain. Like living things, the swells pressed their sides against the canoe and lifted it high onto their shoulders, releasing it to be gathered on the shoulders of others. It's a game, he thought, simply a game that will soon end. Tawhiri-ma-tea toys with me as a dog toys with a rat, and when the rat is dead, the dog becomes bored.

As dawn arrived the rain slackened and stopped. The eastern sky just before sunrise held no hint of red patches that often signal more rain. Against the brightening sea hung long narrow clouds. Their edges pointed up, a sign of calm weather.

He was cold and very tired, and welcomed the sun's heat on his skin. If only there were food. The storm had ripped away the pandanus mat over his provisions and washed them away. A few soggy pieces of sweet potato remained, but they would be too salty to eat. He finished bailing, leaving the remaining water to evaporate. The swells were still huge, but a gentle wind had softened their white tops. He refitted his lines, and the canoe hove to the southeast, into the rising sun.

On course once more, he searched the canoe, finding two coconut shells filled with water and two ripe coconuts. And the stone, which not even gods could eat. Without rain he would die of thirst. At least the lures were safe. He yanked the lines, feeling them tug against the wake. The flesh of fishes is less salty than the sea. You could eat a fresh fish without fear of dehydration. So his plan was simple: fish the lures day and night, hope for rain, and continue on a southward course.

As the swells diminished he compensated as usual for leeway, keeping the bow pointed as sharply into the wind as possible. In seas of reasonable size, the sailing master can estimate leeway and compensate for leeward displacement by observing the angle between his heading and the wake of the canoe.

That night he sailed under clear skies, trailing lures that caught nothing. His stomach complained loudly about its lack of food. After taking two swallows of water he settled back to wait, because waiting was his only choice.

You are always impatient, Hiiaka scolded. He saw her bending at the waist and shaking her finger. So impetuous! The gods made you a mere mortal, not one of them! So be patient. Then she smiled. It's enough, he said to himself. Early next morning the stars *Ke Ali'i o Kona i ka Lewa* and *Hokulei* set together. He was closer to the invisible line dividing the northern and southern worlds.

When the sun was overhead he tacked again. The sun was unkind, paying no attention to his thirst. It burned ruthlessly, keeping the rain clouds away. He finished the half-empty coconut shell of water and tossed the vessel overboard. Only one remained. No birds crossed overhead; there were no sounds except the slosh of the sea against his hull and the clattering of the sail.

Just as the sun was disappearing he caught a *máhimáhi*. It was a large male fish resplendent in greens and yellows. He killed it quickly and ate strips of flesh from its sides, saving iridescent pieces of the bony head to bait his lures. In the fish's upper stomach was a fresh flying fish. He ate this too, savoring its oily taste. The meal alleviated some of his thirst and all of his hunger. He stored what was left of the fish underneath the pandanus mat and rinsed his hands in the sea. As he was starting to tack he heard Hiiaka asking, I wonder, does all food taste the same to you? It seems you swallow everything too quickly to taste it. Ah, but no matter, let me touch your cheek. Here, I've saved you an extra portion . . .

At dawn the next day he drank half the remaining water and ate most of the leftover fish. To ration anything was foolish, he told himself. He was old and needed strength merely to keep the canoe on course. And besides, the haze could return at any moment, then he would not know whether he was alive or dead, except in the way that a fish knows, or a bird. Incredibly, he would not recognize his own hands and feet; his arms and legs would appear to him as mysterious as the stars. And his face, reflected in a quiet pool, would be that of a stranger, no one he had ever known. If the gods decided he should live, they would provide. If not . . .

The *newe-newe* that day hunkered low on the horizon. Perhaps they are resting from the heat, he told himself. Maybe they will call other clouds, and among these some might bring rain. It was water he needed most. He looked around. There were no vessels left in which to hold rainwater except the canoe itself. Were the rainstorm accompanied by strong wind and high seas, sea spray would poison the rain with salt. He hoped for a heavy rain with little wind.

Evening brought no sign of rain clouds. The last of the provisions had been consumed. He could do nothing except hold course and hope to arrive at his destination before death found him.

He felt disoriented. Hunger, he told himself. The sea sliding underneath caused him to lean more than usual; the jostling made staying seated difficult. His arms seemed light, as if they could lift off at any moment, like the wings of a bird. Stand up and soar! And why not? Was he not a child of the Ancestors? He stood suddenly, releasing the sail line. The canoe skidded and spun, dipping its prow under the chin of a swell and causing him to come unbalanced and crack his head against the mast. Spots of color flashed like fireflies against the night sky.

He stumbled to the stern and grabbed the line, pulling the sail taut and forcing the canoe back on course. Stupid! he said to himself. The hunger did not matter, nor the loneliness. A man in a canoe has no companions. His fingers have each other; his hands, arms, legs are paired, not going anywhere without the other. Is the remaining arm of a one-armed man lonely? He could not know, having never met a one-armed man. Ah, but the head! The head is alone. Perhaps this explains the mind, why it questions, doubts, sees ghosts, turns delusional. Yes, those other parts of the body still function when his mind enters its fog: the legs surely walk, although aimlessly; the fingers splice line for no apparent purpose. They remember their tasks, even after the mind abandons them. But the mind can't be fooled. It knows that laughter is bereavement, that love is a form of dying.

In the night he passed the invisible boundary between north and south. *Hokupa'a* lay at eye level; two other stars, *Kaulia* and *Ka Mole Honua*, crossed low on the horizon in the southern sky. At dawn a great fish took one of the lures, breaking the line. His spares had been washed overboard in the storm; only one still trailed behind. Fish by yourself, he told it. Don't look to me for bait, but do your job. Either catch a fish or we both die, and you will sink to the bottom too. The coral will grow on your shiny surfaces, turning them dull. Silt will bury you. He laughed out loud.

Morning came, and the sky was clear and hot. The sea spray felt good on his shoulders, like oven stones when raindrops strike them . . . water dripping from Hiiaka's fingers . . . the dew falling slowly off *pikake* blossoms. He must not think about water! Stupid! he said aloud, and beat the heel of his hand against his forehead. He tacked, not caring how far he had come on the present course, not caring . . .

We are alone inside ourselves. Truly alone. For a time, so short, we can touch others. In love, we think we know someone—think we can see inside another being—but it's delusion, a dream. We touch as if dreaming. Five fingers, ten. Would twenty be better? This traveling and going nowhere; planning trips, never arriving.

It was my failing, not yours, my sterile seed sprayed against your fertile earth. No! I'm a barren rock swept clean. When your seed falls on me I incinerate it; my womb is like hot lava. Nothing matters, not now.

The stone! Why did you do this, Hiiaka? We were going to a new land. The gods there are fertile, the women waddle down dusty paths holding their bellies, men's penises drag along the ground, like Tangaroa's. Babies are conceived merely by touching, you'll see. So . . . Why did you do this? You might have tried! Those silvery bubbles squeezed from your lungs by Tangaroa's hands, they were my last sight of you. When I touched them they came apart.

At sunset a brown moth landed on the side of the mast. It stayed there, hunkered down against the wind that tried to blow it back out to sea. What air currents had brought it? In the darkness he dozed, feeling the sea and relying on the swells to steer. His mind roamed. He awakened once again in his hut, seeing the moth overhead. The lizard's eye seemed empty of curiosity or pity. It was just an eye, unconnected to a mind. He awoke suddenly and reached for the moth, intending to eat it, but the moth was gone. Here he was, following the rhumb of a star that seemed no more real than his memory of Hiiaka.

No rain fell, and without water his mind drifted, entering its fog more frequently and staying longer each time. Nothing could be done about it, although the course held. He passed the first sea-mark, a place where sea jellies gathered in uncountable numbers. At night the surface glowed greenly with phosphorescence. As his prow cleaved through them they shouted to him. Find her! She's Tangaroa's wife now, but she waits for you. After all, Tangaroa has many wives; he won't miss one wife, more or less.

That day he sailed through the sea of sharks, the second sea-mark. In the low swells he could see their eyes reflecting sunlight, their blue backs brightening the deeper indigo of the sea. They swam towards him from all around, jostling each other and bumping his canoe. She's here! they said. We let her pass. Yes, she sank through our midst with a stone tied to her ankle; it happened quickly. Let her pass! Tangaroa had shouted from below, so we had no choice. You may pass too. Sail on. You know the place.

In the night he entered the region of the third sea-mark where flying fish flew only in pairs. The sky was clear, and in the moonlight he saw them rise out of the sea, beating their fins like wings. They spoke to him and said familiar things. Was it memory speaking or Hiiaka giving instructions? Two landed in the canoe. He picked them up gently and dropped them overboard; these were her messengers.

The next day the wind stopped completely, and the swells lay down on their sides as if entering sleep. He recognized where he was. By dawn of the next day the stars 'A'a and

Nana-mua would set together. He stood uncertainly, legs and back aching, and dropped the sail line. The sail hung limply, like a broken bird. Now he would wait. The fog came once more, and he entered it gladly. At dusk the dolphins appeared, his fourth and last sea-mark. They swam around the canoe huffing softly. Like the flying fish they swam in pairs, hundreds of them, each pair rising to breathe as it passed heading southeast. The fog thickened.

Hiiaka! So, you're now a wife of Tangaroa. I hope he's given you many children. Do any resemble me, an ordinary man, or do they all have fins and swallow air from the sea? I've loved you all these years, many years . . . the number escapes me. Half the lifetime of someone who grows old and whose body aches. Do you remember the firelight? Are there fires where you are, ovens of stones in the ground under the sea? I'll eat a lot of baked fish, unless the fishes are all your friends. We'll laugh, as before. Are you cold, Hiiaka? Can you recall the rain on your skin?

The sea is so calm, the whole sky lies mirrored in its surface. The constellations, they're all in front of me, Rangi's universe. One stone will send it reeling. The black circles I make will stride outward, lifting the canoe and breaking up the stars. If I see demons while awake, I am mad, but if I see them in sleep, I'm merely dreaming. Which is this? The stone is tied to my ankle; the sail hangs motionless. Here I stand, Tangaroa, another maker of silver bubbles. Come squeeze my chest.

POND MEMORIES OF GOLDIE

Yo man, take you hands offa me, hear? Why you roustin' me? What I done? I jes hangin', it a hot night, man, know what I'm sayin'?

I jes coolin' off, gettin' wet, know what I'm sayin'? You ain't gotta cuff me, muthafuckas, I ain't runnin' nowheres. I ain't guilty. I dint do nothin'.

Yo scuzzy-fuzzy—where you hair, man? You a brother, ain't you? An' you bald! Shee-*it*. Man, you oughta have a fuzzy haid, you the fuzz.

An' you, whitey five-oh. You got eyes like on a muthafuckin' chicken. Pluck, pluck! Bet'chew got chicken skin too, no lie. When you shit, you prob'ly be shittin' chicken shit. Ha! Salt an' pepper pigs inna black an' white poke. Why ain't you out catchin' bad guys?

Me? Doan be sayin' I jes a smart-ass an' watch my mouf. You know who you talkin' to? A impo'tant dude in this 'hood, thass who. Ax anybody.

Know what I got home in my closet? Paira sneakers, man, wurf two bills, know what I'm sayin'? Wurf more'n you whole five-oh suit, man! New pair ever' week, if I want 'em, ten pair, doan matter.

Hell, I be a rapper, a poet, gonna be famous, maybe tomorrow, maybe sooner. Thass right. The girls, they love me now, they do. I get alla pussy I want, man. They all beggin' fo' it. Them older girls even—eighteen, twenny—they take one look at this here donkey in my pants, they go crazy. They lustin' after me alla time, bro. S'truth. I ain't *bool*-shittin'. Even you momma, cracker five-oh. She allas callin' me axin' fo' it.

Hey! Hold it, man, I jes a kid, no smackin' me around, hear? I get a lawyer on you ass. You know 'bout *po*-lice bru-*tal*-ity, sucka? You doan go smackin' around the brothers, know what I'm sayin'? You gotta couth up, man, live right, get lotsa pussy an' chill, know what I'm sayin'? So relax. I still a juve-nile. I dint live no fo'teen years to get whacked by no ugly cracker.

Hey, listen up, I give you a small rap sample 'cause you ain't worthy of a en-tire show. You gonna remember this someday, tell you gran'chillen. You tell 'em you seen me befo' I be famous, know what I'm sayin'?

Hand me you nightstick, cracker. I pretend it a microphone. Give a show right here. No? Whatsa matter, 'fraid I thump you haid? 'Fraid I raise it up an' whomp you ass? So wha'chew be scared of, I jes' a kid. Okay, you the man, keep you night-stick. Sit on it, ride it on outta town fo' all I care.

Now listen up, hear? An' try shufflin' along wid me, even if you ain't got no rhythm, huh?

> We cain't afford no *in*-stra-ment
> So rappin', it be heaven sent
> Jes let whitey run an' hide
> If he the one ain't satis-fied.
>
> He look at us an' he can tell
> Homeboys in this 'hood is hell
> He look at us an' see the knife
> He runnin' hard, an' fo' he life.
>
> The night it dark, it gotta be
> He think like us 'cause he not free
> We got him now he ain't too far
> The 'hood our home an' this be war.

So wha'chew think, muthafuckas? Rhymin' tight, huh?

But where you rhythm at? We try some mo'. Listen up an' watch my moves, know what I'm sayin'? Gotta catch the flow or ain't nobody 'cept white girls gonna wanna hang wid either o'yo' asses. Okay, here we go:

> Gonna set it straight, cain't sit around an' wait
> Fo' that fox no mo', gonna walk right out the door
> No standin' in the kitchen
> Puttin' up wid all the bitchin'
> An' the lyin' an' the cryin'
> She allas gotta say, "Hey sugar, please stay"
> Then she loungin' at my side
> An' steppin' on my pride
> When I hangin' wid my friends
> An' we be jivin', high-fivin' . . .

Hey, thass good whitey five-oh, you gettin' it, yeah! Lift them big redneck feet! Move that scrawny ass!

Yo bro, you ain't cookin'. Wha'sa matter, you got white blood? Some whitey down onna plan-*ta*-tion poke you granny? You momma, she look like cotton? But the flow be tight, oh yeah!

Okay, that do it fo' now, but y'all gotta practice, wanna work this 'hood, know what I'm sayin'? The brothers, we gonna whup you asses if you ain't got it down.

Say, y'all know Sylvia who live on Thirty-fo'th an' Green? Well, man, she a fox. She got sexy eyes an' big hummers that stick way out. I wrote that poem fo' her. They's mo', but you ain't gonna hear it.

Sylvia, she be twenny, but she love my ass. She hug me alla time an' rub them big hummers on me, an' she be givin' me alla pussy I want, know what I'm sayin'? She allas shakin' an' bakin'.

Sylvia tell me I be famous soon an' she gonna be my groupie when I be travelin' wid my band, know what I'm sayin'? Doan want no strange foxes makin' it wid me, dig?

Wha'chew mean I be changin' the subjeck? What subjeck you be talkin' 'bout? Wha'chew ax me anyhow?

Oh, what we be doin' here, yeah, okay. Me an' Raffie an' Whistle, we hangin' by the pond. We wasn't doin' nothin' special, jes hangin'.

Then Raffie seen this fish. It look up at him outta the weeds, an' Raffie swore it had titties hangin' off of it. An' Raffie doan lie, at least not much. He alla time lie to he momma an' sister, but he doan lie to his homies, know what I'm sayin'? He be dissin' us, we stomp his ass good, know what I'm sayin'? We make that boy pay.

Wha'chew mean *I* lyin'? You fuckin' five-ohs allas interruptin' a man befo' he espress hisself. I ain't finish yet. I be finish yet? You hear me sayin' I finish?

We *wasn't* swimmin'! We was tryin' to catch this fish. I'd of tole you, but you dint let me finish. Shee-*it.* You gonna let me finish?

Anyhow, me an' Whistle we look down an' it be God's honest truth, what Raffie say: that fish be sportin' big ol' hummers. Onna woman, them hummers a size fifty, I swear.

So I says to Raffie an' Whistle, we gonna catch that sucka, then we get us a fishbowl an' charge a dollar a feel. Put out a big sign inna 'hood. Believe it, ever'one wanna come an' squeeze a little soggy nipple, know what I'm sayin'? Man, we be famous, inna paper an' all, on TV too, no lie. We even gonna be on CNN. Bernard Shaw, man, he love this kinda shit.

I gotta do alla thinkin' fo' this trio. Raffie an' Whistle, they dumb-asses, know what I'm sayin'?

Drugs? Wha'chew you mean, *drugs?* Man, when you see *drugs* under the water? You sayin' I be fishin' fo' *drugs?* We doan do no *drugs,* man. I look fucked up to you? Wha'chew mean, *drugs?* I dint see you wearin' no frogman suit.

I tole you, we jump inta that pond to catch us a tittie fish. It be a sorta yella-type fish, lighter'n them other goldy ones. Had skin lookin' light an' daid, like you skin, cracker five-oh. Chicken skin. Watch it! Watch you hand. I sue you ass you touch my handsome self.

I doan know no lawyers? Doan'chew bet nothin', sucka, take

food outta the mouf o'yo' babies, you do. We got us a good
lawyer inna 'hood, man. Doan charge, neither, not fo' the
brothers, know what I'm sayin'?

He get Whistle sister off fo' hookin' jes like that, no problem. Thass what he say alla time, "no problem." He got so
many law books you need a movin' van. You ain't seen so
many books. An' he know what inside ever' one, know it
front an' back, know what I'm sayin'? Man, he take them
other suits befo' the judge an' kick they ass, no lie. They
meat, thass all. So you watch out, doan lay no hand on my
pretty self, know what I'm sayin'?

Why they run, Raffie an' Whistle? 'Cause you the *po*-lice,
muthafucka! Brothers, man, they allas run, see that black
an' white.

Me, I let you catch me. I be fast, sucka, I run so fast I be the
fastest dude runnin' in this town—maybe inna whole world if
I wanna be. I kick *all* they asses. You laughin', huh? You ax
you'self, you be seein' any cracker runnin' pro-*fess*-ional
lately? Shee-*it*. Us brothers leave you ass inna dust if we take
a mind to, no lie. I *let* you catch me, muthafucka, or you be
suckin' my wind, chewin' on dust, know what I'm sayin'? You
too, Baldy, you too fat, be chasin' us young brothers around
inna projects.

Wha'chew sayin', I be drippin' mud on you squad car?
Fuckin' black an' white, man, hunka shit. I doan give no rat's
ass fo' no fuckin' black an' white, man. Them ain't my
colors, know what I'm sayin'? You like a damn woman, wor-
ryin' 'bout mud an' stuff.

I tell you why he name Whistle, now you ax. It easy. That
boy whistle like a angel, oh yeah. A holy sound come outa
them tuneful lips, fo' true. Ol' Whistle, he whistle up jazz you
want it, or he whistle somethin' sof' an' slow. He even
whistle rap, we ax him to. Hip-hop, reggae, it all pass by
them lips.

Yo cracker. You thinkin' the angels all be white, yeah? All
them Christmas-tree angels, they all wid a roun' mouf, like
they got they lip around somebody donkey, prob'ly a brother.

Well, you wrong, sucka. Look above you haid. Thass right,

at the sky. Wha'chew see? You dint see no *black* angel, right? An' why is that? 'Cause they invisible at night! Man, you a dumb muthafucka!

We go check out the pond, maybe see that fish, wha'chew say? Anyhow, you already be parkin' here, takin' up space where the brothers playin' dice, know what I'm sayin'?

Yeah, right here. Shine you light right here. That fish here somewheres, you gotta trust me.

Wha'chew mean 'bout all mermaids bein' white? You been watchin' too many Disney movies, man. They black ones too, you jes ain't seen one. This here one be almos' white, yeah, but they prob'ly a black one in this pond somewheres. Cain't see the bitch at night, know what I'm sayin'?

Hey, I find it! Yeah, down there! You see? See them titties hangin' off of it? Oh, man, wish I had me a net. You believe me now? I be tellin' you, my man, you gotta respeck me.

Yo cop! Wha'chew doin' onna *po*-lice radio? We doan need no mo' five-oh, man, I kin handle this fish. Shine you light on that sucka an' I catch 'im easy. We all be rich. I cut you muthafuckas in, ten percent each, you like that? Jes hold you light steady, doan be wavin' it.

Stand back? Me? Why I gotta stand back? Why I gotta stand back, muthafucka? You crazy, bro? Whose side you on? You a black man too. I gotta career, man, lotsa women I gotta keep happy, know what I'm sayin'? Them sisters, man, they countin' on me fo' stud service.

Hey, tell you what, let me catch that fish while you partner talkin' onna radio an' I give you twenny percent. You an' me, we go on TV live wid Larry King, man. We take our fish an' show the viewers them hummers hangin' down. Make us famous, no lie. Maybe get us inna movies, know what I'm sayin'?

What that boy want now? Why he allas interruptin' a brother when he espressin' hisself? Someone oughta whup his ass, learn him some manners.

Wha'chew mean you got patched to the *mu*-seum? Who you know up at the *mu*-seum? You ain't never been inside that place.

Me? I ain't been there neither, but I be disadvantaged.

Tell me that part agin, muthafucka. Them *is too* titties! I
seen 'em. You fuzzballs seen 'em too. You dealin' here wid a
man who been around, know what I'm sayin'? I seen all
kinda titties—black ones, white ones. I even seen Chinese
titties. So doan be handin' me no *bool*-shit, okay?

What that *mu*-seum muthafucka know 'bout the subjeck?
Why he workin' nights?

Yo man, I ax you a question. You dealin' wid a citizen here.
I be payin' you salary soon's I get me a job. You give me
some respeck, hear?

Say what? English, man, okay? Doan be barkin' out no white-
folks jive-talk fulla big words that doan mean nothin', know
what I'm sayin'?

You tellin' me them ain't titties, they neo . . . huh? They a
neo-*plasm*? An' this here neo-*plasm* is a kinda cancer? Holy
shit. Me an' Raffie an' Whistle, we gonna catch cancer outta
that pond? We ain't? Good, 'cause we don't need no cancer,
thass the damn truth.

So now you sayin' they *ain't* titties. The *mu*-seum know this
shit, huh? Hey, you laughin' at me, you ugly white muthafucka? Why you be laughin'? I say somethin' funny?

Shee-*it*, you prob'ly gonna come catch that fish you'self an'
go on Larry King wid a buncha *mu*-seum assholes, make
lotsa money an' shaft the brothers.

Yeah, I leavin', doan worry, I be outta here. But I comin'
back inna mornin' to check out my fish. I better not be seein'
you ugly face on TV, man, you in deep shit, know what I'm
sayin'?

Okay, okay, I be gettin' my ass home. Hey, how 'bout a
ride? Be tight comin' home inna black an' white. Can we turn
onna siren? Wha'chew mean I all muddy? You ain't carryin'
me, huh?

Well, fuck you then. See you around, fuzzballs. Go lookin'
fo' titties on a pigeon. Yeah, you let the bedbugs bite too.

MUTATION TUGS THE HEARTSTRINGS

THERE IT WAS ON THE FRONT PAGE OF THE NEWSPAPER, RIGHT BELOW the fold: a color picture of a frog with four hind legs. The frog was small, I could tell, because the grubby palm on which it sat was attached to a ten-year-old boy. "He can't jump so good," the boy was quoted as saying. "Even with all them legs."

I sat up in bed. Angst's bare knee, smooth and tanned, rose like an exotic island above the jumbled sea of sheets. I tapped it. "Look," I said, "a six-legged frog."

"That's disgusting," Angst replied, not lifting her eyes away from the comics. She moved her knee slightly, a signal to quit bothering her. I peeked between her hands and saw Buttsie the Cigarette testifying before Congress.

"This is serious," I said, making my voice sound serious.

"Shut up," Angst answered. "It's just a frog."

I set down the paper and watched the ceiling fan creak through its revolutions. The fan is located directly above my side of the bed. The mounting seemed to be loose. I made a mental note to fix it before the spinning blade dropped on me and lopped off a toe, or worse. I noticed how the ceiling itself was stained from an old roof leak, but decided not to say anything.

Angst glanced over and saw me looking up. "When are you going to paint the ceiling?" she asked, and gave the comics a karate chop to straighten a crease. Her other knee appeared above the cottony waves. I pictured the island of Surtsey rising suddenly out of the sea on November 14th, 1963. "Your knees remind me of Surtsey," I said.

"You're weird," she retorted.

"It happened just south of Iceland. Pop! And there it was."

Angst was named Angstrom by her physicist father, whose elemental particles had commenced the next phase of their personal rebirth some five years ago. He had been a slightly built, buck-toothed man with a satyr's eyes, and I had liked him immensely. We shared several traits, including a fondness for laughter and good wine, and a tendency to cower before his strong-minded daughter. Angst it often was, literally—and in my case, still is—but we endured.

"I sense fresh welts on your back." the Professor might whisper when we arrived at his house. "Don't take my impending avoidance of you personally, but . . ." and he gestured at his own back. As Angst moved ahead of us into the living room, I would glance at his angled eyebrows and caprine teeth, and wonder what his feet were like. Although I never saw him without shoes and socks, Angst guaranteed five toes to the foot, offering her own as ontogenetic evidence.

"Doesn't ontogeny recapitulate phylogeny?" I asked Angst, dusting off Ernst Haeckel's discredited axiom that an embryonic vertebrate passes through abbreviated stages in which certain developmental features mirror those of amphibians. I envisioned vestigial gill slits and tails—the human embryo as transient frog—or had we already taken a detour up some attenuated alley of evolution, soon to be asphyxiated in our own fouled waters? I shuddered and gulped air.

Angst slammed the newspaper down on the bed. "*What* the hell are you talking about? And stop hyperventilating."

"Your dad. Are you sure he had ten toes, not hooves? That is, five toes on each foot, not six and four or seven and three. I never did see his feet."

There was a plate tectonic shift of mattress as Angst stood up. "You want more coffee? If so, hand me your cup. *Now.*"

Her brown islands and the overhead white cloud of her rear end disappeared down the hall.

I looked at the picture again. I couldn't take this frog to Calaveras County and expect to win. The kid said it was a poor jumper. However, I might win bets on how many legs it had, which reminded me of a joke. A man with three testicles went into a bar and laid down a ten-dollar bet that he and the bartender had five balls between them. The bartender leaned over and whispered, "I wouldn't make that bet unless you've got four."

Angst returned. "I wish I had three balls," I announced.

Angst rolled her eyes. "Bored, are we? Today is Sunday, the season is spring, the weather sunny and warm. So what do we do?"

"We go looking for frogs," I said. "What else?"

"Lots of things," and she threw back the sheet revealing an entire continent of contoured hills and shaded valleys.

By mid-morning we were out of the house dressed in jeans, hiking boots, and flannel shirts. I was wearing a Key West baseball cap for good luck, which probably worked better on bonefish than frogs. I envied Angst hers with the image of Kermit above the bill. As we were leaving she stopped and adjusted her cap in the foyer mirror, tucking wisps of blonde hair up underneath Kermit's splayed feet. The subsequent application of lipstick led to additional adjustments.

"We're only looking for frogs," I said.

"You never know who else might be out there," she replied, and smiled brightly at my reflection. "Maybe I'll get lost in the woods and have to be rescued." She checked her front teeth for lipstick and, finding none, ran her tongue over them for good measure. "Okay," she announced, "lead me to these mutated frogs, and if I retch it's your problem."

The newspaper had pinpointed Pachaug State Pond as a hotbed of amphibian deformity, and the environmentalists interviewed were using its message to promote a futuristic snapshot of our own species. No handbasket bound for hell was leaving without me, and anticipating how many appendages might eventually sprout from my unconceived children seemed vaguely relevant, assuming direct extrapolation from swamp to delivery room. Actually, I had always feared cyclopianism in any progeny of my own, the single eye staring out accusingly from the crib. But maybe multiple legs were the future, in which case Pachaug's frogs were not an opportunity to waste.

Angst put her Timberland-booted feet on the dashboard as we bounced down the driveway. The treads of the soles were clean, having never touched the dirty ground. "You owe me, buster."

I glanced into her large blue eyes and Kermit's beady ones. "How so?"

"For tolerating this woeful expedition to look for defective frogs. Dinner, at least. *Cuisses de grenouille*, one pair to the frog. And a bottle of cold chardonnay, price being no object."

"I'm thinking about our children," I answered. "The situation could be catching. We can't be too careful."

"We don't have children exactly *because* we're too careful." She glared at me.

"I don't want any *future* children born with four hind legs," I said. "Unless they're twins, of course, or shaped like this." I reached over and grabbed her thigh.

"What the hell are you doing?"

"Feeling angst," I said with a chuckle.

"Very funny," she replied. "That's not exactly a new pun."

"Oh?" I said, lifting my eyebrows. "Who else uses it?"

"Just about everyone," she answered, and jabbed me in the ribs.

"Hey, cut it out, we're on the highway!" We were weaving diagonally across our lane. I squeezed her leg again just as a fat man driving a fatter Buick passed on the left. One hand cradled a telephone, and to give us the finger he was forced to let go of the steering wheel.

"Behave," she admonished. "You're going to cause an accident."

Pachaug State Pond is big, more of a lake than a pond. The trees were just starting to leaf, and the woods still retained winter's twiggy appearance with lots of gray bark showing through. We parked where the signs told us to park and got out. The day was almost too warm for flannel, but we wore tee-shirts underneath. I reached behind the seat and pulled out the knapsack with bottles of water, sandwiches, and a field guide to the North American amphibians.

"Hear that?" asked Angst. "Frogs, for sure."

I listened. "Sounds more like starlings to me." Just as I finished speaking, a small flock of them landed on the other side of the lot and continued making the same noises. I grinned widely and spread my arms in a forgiving gesture.

"Fuck you," Angst said irritably.

We set off single file down one of the trails bordering the pond, tiptoeing around boggy places green with skunk cabbage and scrambling up and down furrowed embankments. In the absence of cover, the trail was bright and airy, packed firm with last year's leaf litter. We tramped through stands of towering white pine and of black oak mixed with birch, coming at last to a small glade. Out of the ground rose boulders of gneiss and schist, smooth and humped like retracted turtles. I dropped the knapsack and lay down. Angst chose to sit on a lichen-covered rock near the pond. Soon there was noise.

"Bullfrog," Angst whispered, pointing at some overhanging vegetation.

I rolled over and got out the field guide. "It says here, *jug o-rum*," I whispered back.

"What?" she whispered.

"*Jug o-rum*," I replied, speaking a little louder. "*Rana catesbeiana*, the bullfrog. When it talks it says, *jug o-rum*."

"Sounds more like *gar-umph* to me," she said, still in a whisper. "The book's wrong. That's a bullfrog, no doubt about it."

I leafed through the pages. "No *gar-umph* in here, so it can't be a bullfrog. Must be an undescribed species. Let's catch it and cut it open. This could make us famous."

Angst turned around to face the water, fluttering her hand for me to be quiet. Suddenly we seemed to be surrounded by frogs, some *gar-umphing*, others strumming or snoring.

"Green frog, *Rana clamitans*," I announced, no longer whispering. "The book says its mating call sounds like a loose banjo string. Do you agree?"

"Okay, a green frog, but that first one was a goddamn bullfrog."

I ignored her. Angst has never been wrong in her life. I thumbed through the book. "Leopard frog, *Rana pipiens*. Its mating call is a sort of snore followed by some clucking sounds."

"Maybe," Angst said doubtfully. "Stop with the Latin names, okay? So, we've heard a bullfrog, green frogs, and leopard frogs."

"Tentative on the bullfrog," I replied slyly. She shot a visual dart my way. "Okay, a bullfrog," I agreed. "Let's go look at them."

We started walking along the edge of the pond, hearing the splashes of diving frogs ahead. There was movement at my feet. I bent down and picked up a small leopard frog. It had three hind legs, the shortest not fully developed. "Hey, look at this."

Angst stopped and turned, seeing what was in my hand. "Wow," she said. "That's really terrible. Maybe the papers are right and we don't have much time left. Humans, I mean."

"I think the newspapers are overreacting." I looked at the frog, pondering what looping tunnels of genetic memory had deposited us all here together. The frog returned my stare, thinking whatever frogs think. It tried to jump, but couldn't, so I set it down. Angst watched, biting her lip. Kermit's expression didn't change.

"What if it looked like a mermaid?" she asked, sounding small. I must have seemed confused. "Our baby," she continued. "What if we had a daughter with gills and a fish's tail?" She turned and started back along the trail.

"What prompted this?" I asked.

"I don't know," she said, not turning around. "Looking at the water, that frog . . ."

We walked on in silence, arriving at the glade after a few minutes. "Do you think it's because of pollution?" she asked.

"Could be. Mutagens in the sediments, cumulative effects from pesticides. Maybe fungi or parasitic worms. Who knows?" Angst unbuttoned her flannel shirt and threw it on the ground, then peeled off her tee-shirt and unsnapped her bra. She sat down and started to untie her boots.

"What's going on?" I asked.'

"We don't have much time," she answered, grinning up at me. Another few seconds and she was naked. I started to undress. "I quit taking the pill," she announced.

"When was that?" I should have been alarmed, but somehow wasn't.

"Yesterday."

"We're pretty close to the pond," I said. "Aren't you worried about mutagens seeping into your bare butt?"

"Right," Angst said. "Get your own bare butt over here and let's make a mermaid."

I knelt, murmuring, "Ontogeny recapitulates phylogeny . . . gills and tails?" Either Angst didn't answer or the mating calls of the frogs were so loud I couldn't hear her.

SEDNA THE SEA WITCH

THERE BEING NO MEDICAL CLINIC ABOARD AN ICE FLOE, HE TOOK UP his hunting knife and cut off the gangrenous toes himself. Qimmiq, willing participant at all gustatory events, gulped them whole like Vienna sausages before settling expectantly on haunches made lordly by the act. But there had only been ten of the delicacies, and Qimmiq's feral demeanor soon crept back, obsequiousness demanding more than a few blackened digits.

In wiping off the knife, he considered if a leg might be next and whether the faunal world could be divided into dogs and their food.

Circling through the falling snow with outstretched arms, staggering on shortened feet, he chanted *ajaajaarniq! ajaajaarniq!* to alleviate hunger, bantering, he knew it, with madness. Human toes converted to dog flesh might yet nourish their original owner. As Da used to say, go hunting with a dog team, because in times of hardship you can't eat a skidoo. He had said it in Inuktitut, but the meaning was clear.

Ajaajaarniq! ajaajaarniq! Can a body consume and nourish itself, and in growing smaller stay the same? *Ajaajaarniq!* Danny Tuk-Tuk laughed, ignoring the dog that bounced beside him and dipped deftly to lick his leaking stumps. He laughed, falling to his knees under thin moonlight, stood over by hunkering stars.

After brushing away some snow, he put his face against the ice and looked intently between his cupped hands, but she stayed well hidden and out of view under the sea. "I know yer down there!" Danny Tuk-Tuk shouted at the ice. "Yer gonner sink me, eh? I see yer soon!"

His mother Mina Sheupiapik had named him in honor of Daniel's visions and Nebuchadnezzar's dreams, a Biblical prophecy, it seemed, of her personal apocalypse. And when they buried her, the remains included two cancerous lungs, a hard liver, and a final black eye courtesy of Da while she lay dying. Then Danny Tuk-Tuk—ten years in the world, newest of four offspring and repository of his family's sensitivity— was given to Naqi, the eldest and his only sister, who finished Mum's job with distracted sobriety. He was fifteen when Naqi's drunken husband pushed her off the back of his skidoo just as it spun out of control. They drowned clawing at each other, desperate to reach air, a rock pasted over with green lichens nearly in reach.

His later rearing fell to Da, who peered out occasionally from the bottle, and later to Docker or Skeezix, whichever was sober enough to notice his presence. Da labored dimly at boilers inside the immense grain elevator that rose like a toadstool from the empty prairie. Inside was a mechanical garden of spinning motors and humming belts, the bruxism of gears. Everywhere, rushing machinery stood ready to ensnare an unbuttoned sleeve or flapping shirttail and draw the soft flesh between metallic teeth. At night, Da's was the only organic intrusion, not counting the rats and the grain.

Deep in this forested interior Da turned knobs, read gauges, and wiped away oil with the rag he always carried in a back pocket—almost like a railroad engineer, except that he never went anywhere. One night a main boiler quit, its pressure dropping to zero. Suddenly, inky darkness such as existed before Tulugaak the Raven pecked through the great bladder that encased the world, letting in light.

Guided by his own illuminated memory and a few emergency lights that came on almost immediately, Da climbed a switch-backing steel ladder towards the telephone. After making the call he gave out too, the pressure of his own pumped fluids dropping to zero just like the boiler's. The supervisor, angry at being raised from his bed in the cold night, stepped on Da when he came fumbling for a light switch, forgetting the power was out. His was a political appointment requiring no useful knowledge. "Shit," he said when he finally located the button on his flashlight. "Double shit."

Da's head was so small and brush-cut that they adjusted the back of his Winnipeg Blue Bombers cap to the first notch. The extra plastic hung limply like a decayed tongue or a translucent tail, visible even in the coffin. At the funeral, Danny Tuk-Tuk remarked how the outsized hat embarrassed him. "Fock it," hissed Docker. "What the fock yer care 'bout Da's hat size?" And he cuffed Danny Tuk-Tuk so hard his ears rang for the rest of the day.

She had been a beautiful but vain girl, admiring her reflection in glassy tidal pools and combing her lush hair with shell combs. Being in no hurry to marry, she rejected all suitors until her aging father, in frustration, chose a husband for her. He was a stranger who arrived in a kayak, face hidden by thick furs and snow goggles of carved whalebone; he promised her similar furs on which to lie and a beautiful house on his distant island. Although she had no wish to leave, her father insisted, so she got into the kayak and her new husband paddled swiftly away.

In high school Danny Tuk-Tuk aspired to write, but his prose was considered too crude—the excessive voice of a primitive. In this he was further discouraged by his teacher, a sharp-faced New Zealander. She was a grimly disappointed woman, braced against the enmity of small failures. Each day brought reminiscences of a Christchurch cottage garden or mist rising from the slopes of Mount Cook. There could be no value in recounting Inuit myths; read Katherine Mansfield, was her advice. Discouraged—drinking, falling to the depths of emotional destitution and disparaging inestimable thoughts—he gave up his single ambition.

"Yer fockin' come to yer fockin' senses," said Docker, pouring them all a drink. "What yer tink, Skee?"

"Fockin' right," answered Skeezix. It was brotherly advice well taken: forget being a writer. What're yer, a fockin' fag? Get yer a job at the grain elevator, be a man.

"Yer short me good on dat drink, bro," Danny Tuk-Tuk said. Docker and Skeezix laughed, and Docker topped up his glass and opened another bottle. They were his family.

He had watched the weather and thought himself well prepared. An Inuk watches the weather, Da had said; he is always looking up. The sky is my map, he tells himself, the roof over my house. I live underneath the sky. The sky had been clear when he tied up the rest of his team on the shore, indicating that the sea ice would freeze solid and be safe. He had taken only his lead dog Qimmiq to sniff out seals behind the drifts. But the ice broke apart under them, the wind rose and the sky descended, and he was suddenly adrift on a floe with Qimmiq and the komatik and kayak they were pulling. In that gale, putting to sea would have been suicidal.

They paddled for days living on dried fish that her husband carried in a waterproof bag. Mountains of floating ice glinted greenly through the mist, patches of green and gold coalescing on the waves like footprints of an incandescent giant. Even as she slept, her husband paddled tirelessly, silently. She didn't yet know his name.

His dying feet no longer burned; in fact, he didn't feel them at all, so distant had they become. He stopped chanting and stuffed them into the kamiks, now too big, and sat down to wait for something. The boots were double-layered sealskin insulated with sea limegrass, but their construction had not saved his feet. The intense cold had diminished, dampened by wet air, and although the wind had dropped, he recognized such conditions as temporary. The island of ice was drifting imperceptibly northeast, ever farther from land.

The last of the caribou meat was gone. Except for the dog, he was out of food and without hope of rescue by anyone he knew. If Docker and Skeezix sobered up enough to look for him they would go to his shack by the river and notice that

the dogs, komatik, and kayak were missing. They would con-
clude he had gone hunting for seals and return to Da's
house, after breaking his lock to see if he had any liquor.
Then in a day or two—if they remembered—they might trail
him down to the sea, but with an offshore wind blowing out
the ice, the sea would be trackless and empty. They might
find his dogs, now lank and starving, staked out by the stone
inukshuk near the small frozen bay and wonder where he
was. Even then . . .

The immediate danger was that a swimming ice bear might
have heard his chanting or Qimmiq's howls and climb silently onto their floe, fur bristling with icicles in the freezing
air and tinkling softly. If he saw the bear in time he might kill
it with his rifle, but hunger was making his eyes play tricks,
seeing two moons instead of one, two of the grinning Qimmiq. The bear would likely kill him instead, but no matter. He
had killed ice bears and always respected their souls. His
soul would be respected in turn.

The kayak was tipped on its side to make a windbreak. The
komatik, still upright on its runners, was his bed above the
ice where he stayed most of the time under a pile of caribou
skins. Qimmiq, starving too, had chewed the edges of the
skins. The sweeping wind had thinned the snow layer so that
constructing a snow house or even a windbreak made of
snow was impossible. His world had shrunk to a space not
bigger than a bleak suburban yard that might collapse into
smaller pieces at any moment. After a last look at the sky, he
climbed under the skins and pulled them over his head.

*More days passed, and she tired of eating the dried fish now
turning rancid; her legs ached to walk. She noticed that her
husband's kayak carried neither hooks to catch fishes nor an
unark with which to spear anything. Always he paddled, stopping briefly for a sip of water from his skin bag or to take a
mouthful of food. She still had not seen his face, hidden as
it was by furs and the snow goggles, and her unease grew.
The only time he spoke was to say, Malingnga! (follow me),
and she dutifully picked up her paddle. Who was this man,
and where was he taking her?*

The stars moved closer, flickering like open flames, shining with the brightness of feverish eyes; there was no ring around the moon. These, Danny Tuk-Tuk knew, were signs of an impending blizzard. After a time Qimmiq started to howl, but soon stopped and curled up beside the komatik. The testing wind lifted and resettled a few hairs along his back and side. He sniffed briefly before tucking his nose underneath his tail to await the storm. In minutes they felt gentle undulations, scouts sent ahead of the swells. Straining, the ice creaked and groaned, and out of the darkness came sharp reports like rifle fire as similar floating islands split apart and the sea washed their remnants clean.

Danny Tuk-Tuk, deep in his kamatik, rubbed the caribou skins gently. Sensation would soon leave his fingers, and he needed to feel this sole evidence of familial camaraderie. The ice floe accelerated out of synchrony with either the force of the wind or the sea's movements. Beneath him, frozen fault lines popped and creaked like rigging strung too tight.

They came at last to a place of calm sea where the mountains of floating ice hung in utter stillness, anchored by their looming shadows. The kayak seemed suspended between sea and air, and the blemishes their paddles made were erased by mist that ebbed and flowed like a tide. Suddenly a cliff appeared, too forbidding to be an ice mountain, and then the kayak scrunched onto a gravel beach. Her husband jumped into the surf and grabbed her arm roughly. Atii! he said, Let's go! She stepped out, heart racing with a new dread.

In February of the previous year, he and his brothers—sober for once by prior agreement—had gone on a caribou hunt, their first outing together. He met them before sunrise at Da's old place, dishevelled now and sagging towards the street. The engine of his skidoo was warm after the short ride from his shack, but the carburetor on Docker's machine was frozen and it took them a half-hour to thaw it. On the way out of the village they stopped at the diner for bacon and eggs and to fill thermos bottles with black coffee and pick up sandwiches.

They rode single file past the grain elevator down the middle of the train tracks that wound interminably west into the prairies of Alberta and Saskatchewan, diverting around switches to prevent jamming their runners fast in the openings.

After five miles they left the tracks and headed west into rougher country, through stands of white pine with branches made secund by the wind. The day was overcast, weak sunlight diffusing pink and orange behind layers of gray stratus. At times light snow fell, obscuring vision, but finally the sun broke out and the sky turned clear and blue. They paused on occasion atop springy bluffs of silver willow folded over by snow while Skeezix scanned the horizon with binoculars.

At mid-morning they tracked south towards the river, finding fields of soft snow perforated by the tips of flat-leaved willow, thickets of bearberry shielding patches of miniature snow willow, sedges now brown and crusty. On low windward rises scoured of snow were mats of black crowberry and the crumpled stems of arctic cotton.

By noon they were fifteen miles from the train tracks and looking east when Skeezix spotted a broken line of caribou moving north. They headed for them, each skidoo pulling a kamatik. Docker jumped off his machine and shot one animal from a hundred yards; the rest scattered, Skeezix in pursuit. Docker's caribou was a male with broken antlers. In the chase a gas can had come detached from Danny Tuk-Tuk's kamatik. He backtracked and picked up the can, then returned to help Docker with the field dressing. Five gallons of fuel had been lost.

Skeezix was there when he got back. His caribou was down a mile east; he had left his kamatik beside the kill. They loaded the skin and dismembered carcass of the first animal onto Docker's kamatik and went to butcher Skeezix's caribou. It was larger, more pale, and also a male. The winter skins weren't the quality of those obtained in autumn when caribou are fatter, but after curing they would make suitable kamatik coverings.

It took two more hours to locate another herd and for Danny Tuk-Tuk to get his animal, but he still remembered the elation. He had killed caribou before, but this one was special. He had gotten it with his brothers. It was female, medium-sized and fat for February, and they dressed it out together, shouting congratulations and extending compliments, vowing to be a family from this moment forth. They stood in a circle and gripped each other's hands, cold and bloody, and Danny Tuk-Tuk cried. Then they sat in the snow and drank thermos coffee and shared sandwiches, recounting the hunt.

They trailed back to the western side of the train tracks just outside the village and cached the meat from two animals underneath stones, heading home with the third carcass and the three skins. They left the tracks briefly to let the six-thirty train through and were back at Da's drinking whiskey by eight. Later they argued, and punches were thrown. Unretractable words of hatred once again became linked to memory, and Danny Tuk-Tuk cried the next day too, but from loneliness and regret. Now, after many months, he felt only a clumsy sorrow. A haunch of the cached meat had sustained him out on the ice, eaten raw and frozen. That was gone, even the bones crushed and the marrow scraped out. Qimmiq had eaten the hoof.

Her husband dragged the kayak beyond the tide line. He pointed up at the cliff and laughed. Unvanga igluga! My house! He pulled off his hood and snow goggles, and she saw that he was old and ugly, with broken teeth. Then to her horror he changed into a bird, a storm petrel. The dark furs became sooty plumage, the kamiks webbed feet, and his shrill laughter blended with the screams of other storm petrels, thousands of them, from their aeries high above the sea. Her husband was not a man, but a spirit.

Danny Tuk-Tuk suddenly became alert. The feet, okay, he thought, but the fingers must not freeze. He needed his fingers. After some fumbling he found the mittens, shoved numb hands into them, and lay down again. Mind departed body and floated upward, diffusing through protracted corridors where events and beliefs came together. Relics of heroes lay on slabs of crystalline ice watched over by stoic gods. At each hero's head burned a lamp of glistening soapstone filled with the clearest seal oil. At his feet were spread delicacies of fresh blackberries, dried caribou meat thinly sliced, smoked char and roasted ptarmigan, and surrounding each were dishes of dipping sauce made of melted fat, blood, and ptarmigan intestine. Laid out on the snow he saw steaming slivers of heart and liver from a newly killed seal.

Voices from the myths nattered on all sides, their intensity rising or falling with shifts in the wind, a nexus of sound made asynchronous by distant chanting of his dead relatives. He could not make out their words. *Tukisiviitt?* they asked him. *Do you understand?* He spoke a reply, but the noise of ice and wind muted the words. *Tukisiviitt?* they asked again and again. *Tukisiviitt? Tukisiviitt?* "I hears yer!" he shouted, pressing his hands to his ears.

She had fainted, and when she awoke her husband was standing over her, an enormous bird with malevolent eyes. At her back rose the wall of the cliff, rough and streaked with ice; in front was emptiness. She pulled her feet back from the edge and peered down at the sea beating itself into froth hundreds of feet below. The skins he had given her to lie on were the skins of fishes, thin and damp, and this desolate ledge was to be her home.

A week after the caribou hunt Danny Tuk-Tuk, having descended to the nadir of self-pity, shoveled out his stove and swept the floor of his shack, feeling in these activities a meager stalwartness. He put the hunting rifle and boxes of shells and his char net into a wooden packing crate and nailed down the lid; the kakivak, used for spearing fishes through holes in the ice, he stood in a corner. He made up his cot and shoved the packing crate under it. The dogs and kamatik, presently on loan to a neighbor who had gone trapping, would be cared for by someone, he was certain. Outside, he winterized his skidoo and tied a tarp over it. Then he packed the few clothes he owned, locked the door, and took the train south to Winnipeg. Two weeks passed before anyone noticed his absence and came looking, and that person was not either of his brothers.

Having never been away from Manitoba he decided to hitch

east, arriving a few days later in Toronto. Being Inuit, he was inured to cold, and slept on a park bench beside a frozen pond surrounded by geese that were strangely calm. They approached him gently, as spirits might, muttering and hissing in spirit voices.

One night he killed a goose and cooked it over a fire ringed with stones. The other geese stood watching, and he saw in the firelight his own image reflected back in their eyes, with prominent nose and chewing mouth. Unnerved, he remembered suddenly that he had forgotten to put a piece of ice in the beak of the dead goose so its soul would have water in the afterlife. He doused the fire and left immediately.

Weeks passed, then months, and her father grew worried. Where was his daughter? Where was the son-in-law who was to help him hunt in his old age? The ice departed, returned, and departed a second time. One summer morning he loaded the kayak and paddled north, hoping to make contact. By sunset the mist had retracted to a low gray reef, and over its rim crept a few stars. He paddled on, arriving after some days among mirrored ice mountains whose liquid valleys were strangely silent, as if owned by spirits. More days passed. His supply of dried char was nearly finished when he came at last to the black cliff. High on a ledge sat his daughter, dishevelled and wrapped in fish skins against the cold wind.

By dawn he was on Yonge Street, where he bought a whore. She led him to a seedy motel and down a corridor made dim by shattered light bulbs. She was white and fleshy and told him that she normally did not have sex with Eskimos, preferring a better clientele. The room was furnished only with a chair and unmade bed. He paid her, feeling oddly perfidious, and they undressed silently, backs turned.

Afterwards he found a bar. Retaining as he did the secondhand appearance of the inarticulate poet or blind artist, he was easily approached. A scrofulous man with bulging eyes bought him a beer and a shot of whiskey to listen to his story.

The man's wife had died many years before and left him her estate. The money was long since spent, mostly on drink, but jewelry worth a small fortune was still locked in the bedroom safe. Her attorneys, knowing his ways, had kept back enough cash to pay annual property taxes on the house and fuel bills to keep the pipes from freezing. He no longer lived there by choice, preferring instead a flophouse around the corner from this very bar. The lock on the safe could be drilled out, of course. The jewelry was rightfully his, but despite being broke he no longer cared. It could stay there.

"She died one night waiting up for me. She had started to write a note." He looked pleadingly at Danny Tuk-Tuk, eyeballs straining against nets of red webbing.

Danny Tuk-Tuk, sunken inside his reverie, made no comment. The man became agitated. He lit a cigarette and blew smoke angrily at the ceiling. "I don't give a rat's ass whether you believe me," he said, waving at the bartender for another round. "Every day I have to tell my story to someone—a stranger—like in the poem."

"To the wedding guest?" Danny Tuk-Tuk asked. They were the first words he had spoken.

The man spun on his stool. "Yeah, like that, smart-ass. Can't you see this albatross?" he screamed, tearing open his shirt. On his chest was tattooed the outline of a large gull containing a woman's name in bold letters. "Can't you *see*, goddamn you?" He stood up suddenly, and there was a revolver in his hand. But Danny Tuk-Tuk was already through the door, running. Later that morning he found the Queen Elizabeth Way and hitched west. He was strangely homesick.

Daughter! the old man cried. Forgive me! Overjoyed to see her father, the girl started to descend the cliff, her fear of falling overcome by desperation to escape. The old man shelved his kayak on the beach, and when his daughter reached him they quickly put to sea. As the old man paddled furiously, she told her story. Hide me, she pleaded, or my husband will surely find us. The old man made her comfortable in the bottom of his kayak and covered her with skins, but it was not enough. They heard the cry of a storm petrel. The old man paddled faster, but the storm petrel flew in front of the kayak and beat his wings against the surface of the sea, raising storm waves. The waves grew large and fierce, and the old man was afraid for his life. Here is your wife! he screamed. Take her! He dragged his daughter from her hiding place and pushed her overboard.

When Danny Tuk-Tuk felt the kamatik shift on its runners, he threw off the caribou skins and sat up. Faint images of Qimmiq scrabbling to retain footing came and went through curtains of snow. The seawater now washing over the ice froze instantly to form a newer, slicker surface. Propelled by wind, ice floes crumpled against each other with the impact of locomotives. This one, he knew, might be next. There was an ear-splitting sound like a tree breaking, and his island was abruptly halved. Qimmiq, nearby a moment before, was suddenly lost from view, his howls drowned by the wind. Danny Tuk-Tuk stood just as the floe tilted sharply to balance itself. He fell to the ice and started to slide, seeing the kamatik begin to move away, slowly at first, then accelerating. He too was accelerating, grabbing for a tiny ridge or crevice, anything.

The girl surfaced beside the kayak and held on. Please help me, Father! she pleaded, but the old man, seeing how the storm petrel continued to whip the sea, took out his knife and cut off the first two knuckles of her fingers. She slipped from view, but to the old man's astonishment resurfaced a moment later. Please help me! she cried, and gripped the kayak once again. But the old man cut off the stumps, leaving her completely fingerless. This time she slipped beneath the surface and did not return. Immediately the waves subsided. The storm petrel, having lost his wife, returned to the black cliff leaving the old man to sadly paddle home, ashamed of what he had done.

Seawater broke over the edge of the floe, slapping him with cold spray. The edges of his ice island were invisible in a gray swirl of whitecaps and snow. He stopped sliding as the ice floe righted itself and lay on his stomach with arms and legs spread wide, anticipating a lessening of movement. Around him no familiar object remained. Qimmiq, the kamatik with his bed of skins, the kayak—all had disappeared.

His daughter had not died but entered a state between life and death. In the liquid valleys of spirits, among the ice mountains, she too became a spirit. Until that moment there had been no marine mammals. Now, the first two knuckles of her fingers became the seals and walruses. The last knuckles turned into the whales and dolphins. She kept them all captive in a clear pool at the bottom of the sea. In her heart burned a hatred for humankind. She was Sedna the Sea Witch, mother of the sea beasts.

Danny Tuk-Tuk felt the cold in his bones, in his flesh where it cut like a steel knife, remorseless and exact. Hypothermia had made him dizzy and confused. Epithets for familiar things became uncertain. Memories of relatives and spirit myths intermingled, and he thought he heard Naqi's voice calling him above the gale.

Suddenly he was a small boy once again, running across the tundra through blooming fireweed and arctic poppies. The fiery colors burned his eyes, and with one hand he wiped away the spray from his face. He heard his answer to Naqi, pictured his laughing mouth. In his hand was a bouquet of crushed flowers. With a loud crack his floe cleaved once more. The section he still held bobbed wildly from the force of the parting, and he found himself again struggling not to slide into the sea.

The voice urgently called his name. Its tone held anguish, as if its owner stood trapped on a precipice. Then reason returned to Danny Tuk-Tuk, and he thought he might be hearing Qimmiq from another floe or wind grating against ice. But he knew it could not be either. It was Sedna's voice pleading with him, begging him to ease her pain. *The sins of humans are the sea lice that crawl over Sedna's body, feeding on her cold flesh. Without fingers, she cannot pick them off or comb her tangled hair. Enraged and in great pain, she summons storms to prevent men from hunting or refuses to release the sea beasts from her clear pool. Then many Inuit starve.*

Danny Tuk-Tuk was no shaman, but perhaps one was not

needed. Was this the beginning, this calling to him? Maybe he, Danny Tuk-Tuk, would assume mythic stature as Sedna's appeaser, descend to the bottom of the sea and pick the lice from her body, inducing her to quell the sea's rage. He, Danny Tuk-Tuk, would assemble her shell combs, shake from them the ooze of centuries and comb her tangled hair, stilling her fury so that the sea beasts might be released for all time.

This was not death—the wolf following. He knew the true wolf, having met in pernicious seasons its lupine inheritors loping across the tundra, pausing to look back aloof and yellow-eyed. Did you walk in front of the stepping death or did the wolf trail you? When you slept, you dreamed wolfish dreams, and upon awakening saw the grinning face lying next to yours.

Dawn was somewhere. He heard Sedna's screams of torment beyond the gale, saw in that scavenging light the sulfurous blaze of her fury. Danny Tuk-Tuk stood up on the buckling floe. "I comin' to yer, baby!" he shouted. "Grab yer hair, I be on my way!"

THE SOMETIME BASS WITH THE GOODLY SET

HE WAS ALL ANGLES AND POINTS AND NO ROUNDED CORNERS. He had lean hair and see-through teeth and in his youth had been known to preach some. For a time he took up serpents with the congregation over in Jolo where anointed ones speak in tongues, prophesying from the depths of strange magnetic fields and shouting out Scripture, Luke in particular, as snakes drip from their limbs like scaled kudzu: *Behold, I give unto you power to tread on serpents and scorpions, and over all the power of the enemy, and nothing shall by any means hurt you.*

West Virginia lacks neither serpents nor enemies, but it has no scorpions. Still, they get by in Jolo, and on that night when the elders stiffened and looked past him, Wallace knew he was no longer in the Word. Following the single drum roll and a scree up the frets by the guitar player, after the chorus of *amens* affirming his lost soul, he came away minus Jesus, with a snake-bit thumb that he sacrificed later to gangrene.

Right now his main concern was starting the outboard and adjusting the mix, a nine-fingered job to which Wallace displayed the usual stoop of impoverishment. There was the cussing, of course.

Onely felt good, like he could have loped all morning under cloud shadows. It must be the Prozac, he thought. He wondered if he would get any sleep with Wallace's stone-bent aluminum skiff wallowing on top of the waterweed like a drowned and bloated hog. A nap was likely impossible, but he was ready to make do. Making do was what he did best.

Onely was rumored to be overly fat, slow of movement, shiny and brown of eye—as Wallace put it, eyes like a couple of wet turds. But Onely cared little about what Wallace thought or said, and rumors passed across him like distorted echoes, barely heard. He felt satisfied inside his eyes, thinking he was well hidden there. A pension out of the mines put food on the table and paid for the cable TV, and a man couldn't expect much more. Still, he regretted with a joyless decrepitude all he had missed in life, whatever that was.

A bullfrog grumped from the bank. On the stern seat Wallace answered with a belch. "I used to be a church-goer," he said, feathering the pull choke with his thumbless hand. "Yessir, I was," and belched again. "But I ain't anymore." He wiggled his ears and seemed horsey and contented despite this confession that was not new. Onely asked himself from which dead menagerie of equine shapes, which peeling merry-go-round, Wallace had arisen incarnate and two-legged, dressed in coveralls that could have fit him double.

When they first met in 1948, Onely told Wallace how things happened to his family in threes, and Wallace laughed until he cried. "Yore name's Onely *Twice*?" His face could be a varicosity even then, run to coarseness by excessive masturbation and the desire to think in parables.

Onely had looked back puzzled as if seeing a Chinaman, but it was true. His uncle Melvin Twice had weighed three hundred pounds and at the funeral six strong men were needed to lift the coffin. When a mine timber fell on his daddy's foot, that foot swole up three times the size of a regular foot and cost his daddy three toes. To this day his baby brother Thrice won bets with those three nipples, and in 1933, Natchez, one of his three sisters, gave birth to triplets. Two died right off, a fact never mentioned by Onely out of a lurking respect for symmetry.

Wallace untied the stern line holding them to the dock and edged the skiff around the lake, parallel to the bank. A cloud of vapid blue exhaust hung beside their faces like personal gas. Their favorite bass hole was maybe fifteen minutes away if the mix was right, but Wallace liked running rich. Usually the engine died like a shot duck, and they sat drifting while Wallace yanked the starter cord, worked the choke like a plunger, and wondered loudly if Mr. Evinrude's parents had ever married.

It was nearly noon, late for bass but not for brim. A punkinseed was better than getting skunked, although Wallace didn't agree. He was a bass man all the way.

"I'm dropping anchor up beside that patch of spadderdock," Wallace announced. It was his boat, leaving Onely no say in the matter. Not that he cared. Anyway, it was where they always anchored.

"Got me a new mail-order reel," Onely said.

Wallace eyed Onely's shiny Shimano as if it might be venomous. "Never figgered you to go Jap," and he spat for emphasis. "I fought the Japs in the Great War." But Onely knew that Wallace had been a guard at a Japanese-American internment camp in California and the only fighting he had done was in the barracks.

Such could not be said of Onely, returning from a hitch in the same war too distant from his special history ever to relive it. Having found the world, he lost his place in it, the confidence of belonging somewhere, and was forever then a nomad in his own house. Erma Jean, half crippled with arthritis and mean as a fire ant, treated him like a boarder, hooting at him from the couch to carry her plate to the sink and wash it. Their yellow cat watched indifferently, sopping up and savoring its own selfishness, nurturing the greater challenge of mice.

His retirement revolved around changing rolls of toilet paper and flicking light switches. She nagged him into cleaning the wallpaper with stuff resembling modeling clay that picked up the dirt and held it, telling him always about coal dust settling off his clothes all those years coming in from the mines. He meekly obeyed, still resigned not to be an inheritor of the Earth. New wallpaper would have been quicker, but Erma Jean loved her tiny pink rosebuds, and by acquiring the new she might have missed out on the torment of monotony. When he complained about how his wife treated him, Wallace smirked and replied, "A man yore age and still pussy-whipped." Onely guessed it was true, although pussy was not a subject that came often to mind.

They stopped and anchored. Onely peered down to where strands of hornwort wiggled greenly, the rumpled surface cutting apart their stems and rejoining the ends with an oscil-latory rhythm. Brim beamed up at him all sappy, like expec-tant commuters.

Wallace was rigging his casting rod. Onely watched without interest, having rigged his own rod before they left the dock. He thought lots about different things, usually ideas he got from reading at the public library over in Bluefield where he went often when the weather was too rainy or cold for fish-ing, or simply to avoid Erma Jean. Just yesterday he had read a travel article in a magazine. The trip took nine hours by jet plane, and that was *after* you got to New York City.

Onely spied a message there and settled himself more com-fortably on the bow seat. He could do this now that the boat had stopped moving. "I hate traveling nowadays," he said, even though he never did. "Traveling's easy on the young, but men our age carry the awful burden of stool softeners and suppositories and foot powder. Nitro tablets." He did not mention the Prozac, which was making him dizzy in the heat. During his last checkup the doctor had told him that he might be depressed, and Onely supposed it was true.

Wallace snorted. "When's the last you traveled?"

"I don't recall, but me and Erma Jean went to Charleston back some time to get her arthuritis looked after." Following a pause, "We took the train." Wallace knew about that trip. He'd known about it since it happened twenty years before.

"The Lord God never promised you a rose garden," he snapped.

Onely pulled his belly up over his belt and watched Wal-lace's spit spread mayonnaise-fashion across the water.

"I see you got new thread too," Wallace remarked. "That come with the reel?"

"Excalibur Silver. Bought it separate. 'That's how you survive the jungle,'" Onely quoted by memory from the original carton. "And new crankbaits, self-suspending. Excalibur Fat Free Shads."

Wallace waved a hand Onely's way and turned his head in disgust. "Well, shit, them bass don't stand a chance against you. No sense in me dropping this old spotted popper over." Onely knew Wallace was relishing the chance to test whose equipment was better, and if Onely caught more fish Wallace would blame it on "advanced technology."

Onely crossed his hands over his belly and considered Erma Jean's admonishment about all literature except the Scripture being gates to trespass. Ever dutiful, he always opened the Holy Book first on settling into a chair at the library, wandering into Biblical deserts alongside raving prophets, marveling at the opaque teachings of Jesus, and emerging from the Four Gospels as if from a thick sandstorm. A thought floated past, and his mind rose to the bait: had Jesus been a committee of scribes unable to reach consensus? Who else except a committee could have rolled away the stone?

When that slipped the hook, Onely said, "I read at the library that fish can see colors, and colors on a lure make a difference."

Wallace considered. "It don't make any difference because the Lord God put fish on this Earth for man's use. It's His way."

"I thought you wasn't religious anymore."

"I ain't, but a man still needs reasons for what he sees." There was a hiatus while they each considered what the other had said—or didn't consider it, in Wallace's case.

"I see you still got on your Jesus belt buckle," Onely said, his lips barely lifting in what passed for a smile.

"Goddammit, don't dig at me, Onely. You know this buckle was give to me by Bernice." To regain the offensive, Wallace peered into Onely's open tackle box and said with a smirk, "Got you some new ballhead jigs."

Onely leaned forward with effort, gasping out a mighty grunt as his diaphragm folded double, and took out a paper bag. "Yep, and here's others." He rummaged in the bag, extracting a mass of tiny jigs, their hooks entwined. "This here's a aspirin-style Buck Shot, a Tear Drop called a Thunderhawk Talon Tear, and two Bullet jigs." He held two other jigs against the sun, one between each thumb and forefinger, and examined them minutely through bifocals as if they were rare clear gems. "This one's a Blue Fox Foxee and over here we got us a Lindy Quiver."

"You aiming to demolate the whole damn brim population?"

"I am and I will," Onely answered firmly, "but I'll leave enough to multiply their kind." He could talk back like this to Wallace even if he couldn't to Erma Jean. It was enormously satisfying.

As if reading his mind, Wallace spoke and said, "Yessir, I reckon they's two differences amongst us, Mr. Twice: I ain't the one in this boat that's pussy-whipped, if you get my message, and I ain't the one that's going to get skunked on bass this day." He cast his faded leopard-frog popper up against the spadderdock and gave a tug to start it swimming home.

Erma Jean didn't approve of Bernice and Wallace living in sin, but Onely didn't care. Having deposited his DNA into several other willing vessels, Wallace had allotted to Bernice the task of burying him. At seventy-nine, he was twenty years her senior. Bernice had come to hold Onely in low regard ever since he told Wallace about the South Pacific islands, where in olden times dead chieftains were cast adrift on ocean currents in their royal canoes. Now Wallace insisted that Bernice bury him in his bass boat, and she had her family to consider.

Bernice was odd-looking, resembling the mismatched halves of a thin woman and a fat one. From the waist up she was spare and bony as a winter tree, her collagen plus whatever fat and life's juices she had accumulated having sunk to the bottom and pooled there. In their house, where outside shadows bent darkly against the musty curtains, Wallace forced the stump of his thumb against Bernice's cracked lips in the morning and again at night. Those who get snake-bit are not in the Word; they fail to carry Jesus. At Jolo, Wallace handled serpents on faith alone, not as under an anointing when the divine hand nudges aside reptilian instinct and the flesh cannot be harmed. That bite was coming. Jesus knew, and so had the congregation. Now Bernice suffered for it.

Onely considered lowering his jig into the water, but the effort seemed too much. He looked over instead and saw a tapering shape, near the boat but still a fair distance out. The object seemed to scull in place, pale against the deep of the lake, neither rising nor sinking, rolling partway over as if looking up at him. There could be no bigger bass anywhere. And it had to be albino.

"I see the biggest bass since the world's creation," Onely said softly.

After a minute Wallace answered without turning around. "I'd call that a *sometime* bass, 'cause you think you see it sometimes when you don't. It ain't there, Onely. They ain't a bass in this whole lake bigger'n two pound."

Onely looked again. The object sank slowly, floating towards the dark bottom before being grabbed by hidden eddies and shifted like a sheet of newspaper blown through an alley. And then it disappeared. Onely sat up and looked at the back edge of Wallace's Caterpillar cap where a horsefly prospected carefully before sinking its shaft. He was rigged for jigging brim; changing over to a bass rig would require some effort.

"Goddammit, don't be shaking the boat," Wallace admonished. I think I got me a trailer here, just inside the spadderdock." Sure enough, a small bass edged out of the weeds, showing interest in the popper.

Onely decided not to mention what he had seen, not out of selfishness, but because a fish to Wallace was just a trophy, something to brag about, and the bigger the fish the bigger the brag. Wallace had no aptitude for the mystical responsibilities of fishing.

Onely looked down again, seeing the hornwort forest arise undulating out of the polysaprobic ooze. He watched for a while, mesmerized by the swaying, not thinking about anything in particular. Strung at the end of his Silver Thread by a couple of hook knots and hanging off the last eye of the rod was a shiny Turner Jones Micro Guppy, looking like itself alone. A what-the-hell feeling came on him, and without moving his bulk he lowered the jig over the side. Nothing happened, either above or below. Every so often Wallace's plug bit discreetly into the water; hovering squadrons of dragonflies arrived and departed. A horsefly fed from between his sweating shoulders, but he ignored the pain. The jig rose and fell, too new and obscene even for the brim, which eyed it suspiciously as residents anywhere will eye the foreigner.

Onely felt light in the head, and his arms and chest seemed to bear a great weight of time. Anticipating what? The day felt suddenly hotter. Must be the Prozac, he thought, but the view had become hazy. Lake and sky joined, their edges held together by the stitching of trees.

He looked down again. From the dark water rose an image that grew larger and brighter, separating abruptly from the curtain of the lake. Onely was astonished. It was a drowned white girl with hornwort hair, green and trailing. Except for the hair she was pale beyond belief, like snow. Her lips brushed the jig, but hers were not disturbing motions. Nothing she did glittered the surface. No, she must be alive, he thought, because her movements came too quick for the dead. She somersaulted as if in play, arching over backward and stretching towards him enormous breasts, alabaster as the rest of her and the size of cantaloupes. No smile crossed the mouth, the eyes seemed blind and colorless, without irises.

Onely felt disembodied, as if sinking into himself, hearing behind his ears a drumming like heartbeats gaining distance.

"I seen something peculiar," he said hoarsely.

"You ain't seen shit," Wallace replied without looking back. "Now shut up and fish."

Onely, the final snapshot of that goodly set lying wet and undeveloped on his brain, sagged back. Abruptly the absence of sound and light came as a sublimation. Time drifted and the bass rose no higher, avoiding open water as if fearful of sunburn. Still facing the stern, Wallace sang the Oscar

Mayer wiener song. The squadrons of dragonflies departed on another mission, but green-bottle flies were just arriving, having discovered in the lolling tongue a disguised entrance ramp to a new nursery. Still earlier arrivals, resplendent in iridescent chitin, were measuring the space between adenoids, possibly for French doors.

It's true that a man weighs more dead. At the dock they needed four strong men to get Onely out of that bass boat and six to lift the coffin on Saturday.

JEALOUS LADY

HE STOOD AT THE PIER'S EDGE AND LOOKED OUT AT THE SEA AS IF for the first time, or the last. His gray hair was cut short, and on that morning he wore a windbreaker as if to insulate some remnant of a private mortality. When a gull settled silently before him he recognized in its demeanor his own torpor, in its ruffled feathers the disheveled peaks of memory.

A boat horn blew. There were voices, swash, a muttering engine. Words made brittle by water skipped across to him like stones and lodged in his ears. They had no meaning. Other gulls descended out of sight calling coarsely, shapes indistinct and merged with the fog. Ballyhoo broke under the pier like raindrops, metallic and intermittent and thin, dissolving after seconds into faint echoes.

You're early, said a voice at his back, and he turned slowly around.

I've got nothing else to do. Anyhow, it's time, he replied, his eyes and face impassive.

Then give me a hand, said the captain. They clumped off down the pier, scuffing the wet planking, walking single file, not speaking.

They boarded a big offshore sportfisher named *Jealous Lady* bristling with fighting chairs and outriggers; the trolling reels had been carefully oiled and their drags set, the scabbarded rods rising vertically into the morning. Dock lines creaked when they stepped onto the white deck. Their shoes left footprints in the dew.

They busied themselves with unpacking and separating the frozen bait, thawing the chum, checking how the rods were rigged, and readying the teasers—bait lines trolled far behind the boat from the outriggers—one bait starboard, one port.

The captain held up a frozen blue runner. If these little beauties don't hunger up a billfish then I'm damned to hell, he said. We also got ballyhoo, everything fresh-frozen and firm. The captain was a large man who huffed as he talked; when he stopped talking his breath blew hard and loud like that of a horse.

The other man did not reply. He squatted and lifted the flowing deck hose from a scupper and rinsed his hands, feeling the pain now burning his guts, knowing that without the pills it would worsen. He had taken a pill earlier, the last one. The empty bottle was at home on the dresser in the room where his wife lay sleeping. Unconsciously his hand touched his shirt pocket.

The pay phone rang. That's for me, said the captain, and he clambered heavily onto the pier to answer it. Yeah, this is Cap'n Red, he huffed into the receiver. Yeah, we're ready when you are. Just waiting for the mate. I told him to stop and pick up drinks and lunches on his way in. He'll be here any minute. Y'all come on over and get settled. Park your car where you see the spot marked off for *Jealous Lady*. He grunted several times in assent, listening. Then he repeated, Y'all come on over. And he hung up.

Here's Benji now, said the captain. Benji! Get the hell over here and give us a hand. Folks are on their way. You got lunches and drinks?

I got 'em. Maury didn't have no ham, so I got chicken sandwiches. Hope that's okay.

It'll do. I'm hoping we'll be so busy nobody will even stop to eat.

Maury says come by and pay your bill or you'll be getting shit sandwiches next time.

The captain laughed and shook his head. That's good. Yep,

that's real good, he said. He laughed again and sucked air through his teeth and said to no one in particular, I ought to write that one down.

The other man's guts were burning uncontrollably. He sat hollow-eyed on the port gunwale and leaned back, steadying himself with his hands. Say Red, you got a Coke or something? I'm feeling thirsty. Maybe a Coke could help quench the fire, maybe not.

Couldn't be all that work you just did. . . . Sure, help yourself to the cooler. Where's your boy? Never mind, I see him.

The boy who emerged from the fog had that shuffle-footed, narrow-headed, jug-eared look desired by the military. He carried a scuba tank over one shoulder and a duffel in his other hand. I got to fetch the rest of the stuff, he said, and set what he had on the edge of the pier. The man put down his Coke and reached for the equipment and lifted it over the gunwale a piece at a time and carried it to the stern and stowed it in a corner beside the cooler, first the tank and then the duffel. When he looked up the fog was lifting and a breeze had found its way in from the sea. The limbs of the big casuarina beside the bait shop were writhing and twisting greenly like tentacles of a hydra.

The boy made two more trips, on the last returning with a third scuba tank and inflated truck tube that had a loose net of heavy mesh taped along its inside edge and draped through its center. He set the tube on the edge of the pier, jumped lightly onto the deck, and lifted the tube aboard. Might as well rig the flags, he said, and reached for a long fiberglass fishing rod that had been converted to a flagpole. From a hip pocket he took a small diver's flag that was red with a diagonal white stripe and fitted through the grommets with swivel clips. By these he attached the flag to eyelets near the end of the pole. From the other hip pocket he took out two crumpled pennants, one international orange, the other bright yellow, and clipped these to the pole one atop the other but below the diver's flag. When he had finished he jiggled the rod into a rod holder taped to the outside edge of the tube and taped the handle and holder together with electrical tape.

The man watched from where he sat on the gunwale. Test the radio and GPS, he ordered. The boy opened a black Pelican case made of heavy fiberglass. It resembled a small suitcase except that when the lid was snapped shut an O-ring set into a groove around the inside edge was squeezed tight against a narrow flange on the body of the case, making a watertight seal. Everything inside was protected; the case would even float.

The boy switched on the radio and turned up the volume. Testing, testing, he said. Come in, come in *Jealous Lady*, come in. The radio on the bridge crackled. Did it work, he asked? You can't hear your own voice. When you call up one of those radio shows you can't hear what you say. Everybody can hear except the one calling in.

From the bridge came, I read you, son. This is Cap'n Red aboard *Jealous Lady*. I hear you loud and clear. His voice sounded strange and distant but still close by.

The boy looked up. Okay? he asked.

Okay, the man said. Did you put in new batteries?

Yeah, they're new last night.

Good. Keep the radio set to channel sixteen. Now the GPS.

The boy took the global positioning system out of the Pelican case and switched it on. It was about the size of a hand calculator. There were momentary flutterings from the LED display while the antenna searched for four of the Navstar satellites circling Earth, and when it found them the latitude and longitude of *Jealous Lady* appeared suddenly on the screen. The man stayed where he was because it hurt to move.

It works good, said the boy.

Seems to. New batteries?

Yep, the boy answered. He put the radio back in its plastic jacket and the GPS inside a ziploc bag even though it was made to be watertight, then he put both units in the Pelican case and snapped the lid shut.

Wait a minute, the man said. You got the flare gun and flares?

Yep.

Show me, the man ordered. He leaned forward, trying not to grimace.

The boy opened the case. Flare pistol, he said, holding it up. And flares. And while I'm rooting around, here's my car keys, six granola bars, six Hershey bars in a ziploc bag, and a canteen with a quart of drinking water. And there's a gallon jug of drinking water I'm fixing to tie to the inside of the tube. In fact, I'll do it now. He stood and tied the jug in place and tested the cap to be certain it was leakproof and secure. Then he looked over at the man and said he guessed they were set even if they had to drift around all night in the Gulf Stream.

Now tie off the handle of the Pelican case with some of that three-eighths-inch line, directed the man. Loop one end around the tube two or three times—same with the handle of the case at the other end—and tie a bowline in both ends and a half hitch afterwards.

The boy grinned. Ain't that overkill? If a bowline won't hold, nothing will.

Just do it. You can't be too careful where we're headed. Not many people dive the Gulf Stream out of sight of land, drifting along like weed in the current. If that case busts loose while we're under, Red won't have a clue about where to find us.

The party arrived just then, a man and his wife dressed in shorts, pale and overweight, perspiring in the cool air. They stood heavy-legged and uncertain on the edge of the pier.

Is this the *Jealous Lady*? the husband asked, although the name was painted in large letters on the stern.

That's us. I'm Cap'n Red and this is Benji the mate, and these two fellers are friends of mine that we're dropping off for a little scuba dive out in the Stream.

The man's brow furrowed and he pursed his lips. This was to have been a private charter, he said, sounding petulant. We paid lots of money for a private day of fishing. You never said anything about taking along scuba divers.

Didn't think it was important. We're dropping them off in the afternoon and picking them up on the way in. Meanwhile, they'll stay out of sight below and you can fish till your arms drop off.

I still don't like it, the husband said. The captain made no comment.

Why not come aboard and have some coffee? asked the captain. Would you like some coffee, ma'am?

I guess so, said the woman. How do I get over there?

You step down onto the gunnel and me and Benji, we'll help you aboard and get you comfy.

The woman looked doubtful, but she took a step towards the boat. Now don't drop me, she said.

When the two guests were aboard the captain made an announcement. I've got to say this, so don't be insulted or anything. But if y'all tend to seasickness then pipe up now. I got seasick pills aboard and it's always best to take them at the dock and not wait until you're feeling sick out there.

The woman seemed about to answer, but her husband interrupted and said they were fine and accustomed to being at sea and not to worry. However, he added, I'd like a cold beer to sort of settle my breakfast if you know what I mean, and if there's going to be any shortage of beer then someone had better go find some more pronto.

After Benji had delivered a cup of coffee to the woman and a can of beer to the husband the captain took him aside and reminded him to keep alert, because it looked like a hard day ahead with maybe two sickies aboard and one of them also a drunk. Benji nodded. And, the captain added, maybe the dive gear should be stowed forward just in the event someone barfs.

As they left the pier a stiffening breeze was driving out the fog and whipsawing the coconut palms, lifting and rattling their fronds. It raised white pustules on the surface of the harbor and as they rounded the breakwall and met the face of the rising sun the ocean sparkled like a starry meadow. The man scanned the deck for his footprints as if by finding them he might evoke some sign of himself, but they had turned vaporous, like deaths forgotten.

When the boat attained cruising speed he went below and

from the hatchway beckoned his son to follow. They sat across from each other on the cushioned seats, knees sometimes touching with the roll and pitch. All around were the rumble of engines and the thudding of the leaning hull.

We've got to talk, said the man. There's stuff that needs saying and there's no time left. I can't wait it out anymore.

What do you mean? asked the boy, suddenly worried. He examined his fingers, pushing back a torn cuticle, not wanting to look up.

Just what I said, the man replied. Your brother and sister were older and maybe I spent more time with them. Then again, maybe I didn't. I was always working at the plant, day and night. Shift work. You remember. He looked away.

The boy nodded, still searching for distraction in his hands.

Anyhow, the pain's got real bad. I can hardly stand it.

What about your pills? The pills help. Don't you take the pills?

Up until today, but we're going diving and I couldn't risk feeling woozy or stupid. The pills make you stupid. They make you want to lay there and watch television or stare at the wall.

Are you hurting now? I mean real bad?

Yeah, real bad.

We didn't have to come. I'd rather of stayed home than see you hurting. The boy looked at him with pain in his eyes and the man thought how this was his own flesh seated there and how the pain he was seeing in someone else was as real as his own, although in a different way.

It's okay. Really. You heard all your life how Red and me made this dive back when we were young and there wasn't all this fancy equipment. We went out with another guy in an open boat and just stepped overboard. The guy, he cut the motor and hoped he wasn't drifting faster or slower than we were a hundred feet down so he'd be able to find us among the swells. And ever since you were little you've wanted to make this dive, right?

I guess so, the boy answered, grinning weakly.

They talked until the boat slowed and they could see Benji move across their line of sight through the open door of the hatch. Then they went on deck and watched the lines being baited and played out and felt *Jealous Lady* swing into the current with chum trailing behind. Black and white laughing gulls dropped down into the chum slicks looking clean and formal against the indigo sea.

When they went below again the man said how he once dreamed that people sought a subterranean labyrinth thinking it was Heaven, a place of endless caves and passages, and they searched by entering openings at the bottom of the sea. When they failed in their searches he watched them bubble back up as if through cracks in the sea floor, and they emerged covered with black ooze. Not here, one might say. I couldn't find it here, meaning an entrance into the labyrinth. And when he had finished he chuckled and the boy looked astonished, not knowing his father dreamed, and asked if there was more to be told, but what he really meant was whether any future moments could be theirs alone.

The man understood and said there had been other dreams but they were difficult to recall except for one recurring dream. This one seemed more real every day, but believing it to be fully true might be dangerous: memory is blind and random, a dredge bumping across the ocean floor retrieving and then losing scraps of information. It was not so much the dreams that matter but a recounting of dreams, their possibilities. Probably everyone dreams, he said, even people without hope. His own dreams had never left him, and he speculated that a man's dreams might be the last to go, exiting at the moment of death after lowering the shades, switching off the lights, turning the key in the lock a final time.

Tell me about this dream, the boy said. The dream that gets more and more real.

I dream about mermaids, the man replied. He shook a finger at the boy. Not the kind you probably think, he added. Not the sexy kind. The mermaids I dream about are sweet and gentle. Where they live, nobody is in pain. There's no hunger or sadness, no discomfort at all, only singing and friendship. It's a different world from this one, and he glanced around the cabin. Yessir, he said, I heard them singing when me and Red went diving out here those many years ago. I told Red, and he said it was rapture of the deep. But it wasn't. I heard their voices all around. I couldn't make out any words, just a melody. I can play it all day in my head, but couldn't hum it on a bet. I wanted to go find them, just slip on down and keep falling, but our time was up and Red was yanking on my arm to go back.

At noon the boy went to the cooler and retrieved sandwiches he had made himself and cold drinks. They sat on the cushions and ate and talked and listened to the engines churn and felt the sea under and around them. The man explained why it was important to know about birds and fishes and trees. It had to do with identity, he said, and anyone who fails to recognize individuality in the world has lost his own place in it. But names are arbitrary. Names are given to us and we give them to other forms of life fully capable of recognizing individuality in their own ways, although not in ours. Different human cultures have different names for the same animals and plants, but this in no way subverts the value of recognition. Distinction accents identity. Can there be black without white?

In mid-afternoon they went on deck and collected their gear. The man who had paid for the charter was asleep in his chair; Benji had removed the rod from his hands and sheathed it. The woman was sick. No fish had been caught.

The captain set the auto pilot and came down from the flying bridge. You're brave, he said, but the other man only shrugged.

Not so brave, he answered.

You know what I mean, the captain replied as if not hearing him. You know damned well what I mean. Shake this old hand. They shook and suddenly there were tears in the captain's eyes. He pulled the other man to his chest and then stepped away embarrassed.

The woman watched dully as they descended through the

hatch to undress. Once below they stripped naked and pulled on thick wetsuits, emerging again on deck. The boy threw the tube overboard after first tying off the tow line on a stern cleat. The tube bobbed and weaved in the swells, and in the exhaust of the slowly turning engines the woman began to retch.

We'll go off the starboard side, the man said, and leave her be.

This marks the spot, said the captain, and he put the engines in idle from the lower bridge. At least a mile to reach bottom. Didn't bring an anchor, did you?

The man and the boy donned flippers, masks, and snorkels and pitched backward over the gunwale. When their heads appeared Benji handed down the scuba tanks, now rigged with regulators and backpacks. They wriggled into the packs and made sure the BCs contained no air. Then Benji handed down weight belts, which they strapped on. After the other gear had been transferred and secured to the tube they gave a thumbs-up. The captain released the tow line and when they had drifted a suitable distance he put the engines in gear and *Jealous Lady* wallowed south, her stern lifting and dipping in a following sea.

The man spit the snorkel from his mouth. Tie on your wrist line, he said. The lines were a hundred-fifty feet long and tethered them to the tube as they drifted a hundred feet down. The added length would keep them from being yanked about when the tube rode up and down in the swells.

Set your bezel, said the man, and they twisted the bezels of their watches to mark the time of descent.

What's your air pressure?

Thirty-two hundred, the boy answered.

Mine too, the man said. We start up slow at fifteen hundred pounds or twenty minutes, he continued, whichever happens first. Drift vertical with your head up and kick just enough to maintain position. Remember that without landmarks we won't know up from down. Watch which way your bubbles go and stay underneath them. Keep looking at your depth gauge because when these wetsuits start to compress we'll tend to sink, not float, and once the neoprene flattens out we'll sink faster. If you feel yourself dropping too quick, give the BC a little jolt of air. Okay, let's go, but swim away opposite me so we don't get these wrist lines tangled.

The unstable surface was causing the tube to buck and wallow. No more talking was necessary. The man gave thumbs-up. The boy nodded and they descended vertically.

Immediately the noise of wind and splash gave way to silence and they withdrew from the upper world as if into a blue cave. Imploding swells drove air beneath the surface, and at first they confused these bubbles with their own ex-haled air. When they looked up after having descended thirty-five feet the ball of the sun had disappeared, the dense jagged plain overhead bent and cleaved the downwelling light and splintered its edges, and they found themselves in a holo-graphic forest of shimmering columns. Beneath them a deep-ening twilight attenuated in shades of purple to the depth of the world. At fifty feet they checked their gauges, keeping well apart. Visibility in the horizontal plane was excellent, and staying in full view of each other was easy. At a hundred feet they turned and gave each other a thumbs-up.

Now that they had taken safety measures, they could look around. In the distance a school of horse-eye jacks swam slowly along a course parallel with their own northward drift, moving ghostlike in and out of view, invisible during mo-ments when the intensity of light reflected off their silvery sides matched the intensity of the background light. Comb jellies were all around, transparent cylinders edged in glow-ing greens and reds. When they held out a hand and cupped one, its outline became indistinct against the unnatural white-ness of skin. A school of dorado raced past on some ances-tral errand, willing a legacy of startled energy and the lin-gering image of green and gold. And once a billfish rushed like a frantic demon out of the gloom, its eyes huge and haunted, its sail flapping like a cape, and what light there was streamed in ribbons from its back, leaving the illusion of a shifting rainbow.

Later the boy's memory would extend this brief time, playing it out languidly and drawing it close; the harsh grief distilled and purified those scenes. At first he felt guilty thinking they might have talked longer, but words would have been superfluous. The gift he received that day was delicate, demanding silence, the ecstasy and foreboding strangely compatible, as if he had spent a lifetime in their company.

They ascended slowly after twenty minutes, coiling their wrist lines, ducking sideways to avoid a cluster of Portuguese man-o'-war trailing invisible tentacles. As they surfaced, laughing gulls bobbed in the troughs of swells as if expecting them, and a squall passing to the east seemed like the curtained entrance to another universe. They untied their wrist lines and wriggled out of the backpacks, clipping the rigs to brass snaps dangling from short lines taped to the sides of the tube.

The boy was ecstatic and spewed forth recollections of what they had just seen, reminiscing even in the short history of the event. When at last his descriptive powers waned the man spoke.

Glad you enjoyed yourself. Now drop your weight belt.

What?

Drop your weights. It'll make floating here on the surface a whole lot easier. These wetsuits give enough buoyancy, and there's always your BC. That lead should fall a mile, maybe more. Think of it as your present to the Stream, a little something you're leaving behind.

The sea was rising, and spray slapping their faces made talking difficult. The boy did as he was told. Aren't you dropping yours?

No, I'm keeping mine.

What for?

I got another dive to make.

So that's why we brought that other rig! I should of brought two. You're going back down alone?

That's right. I heard them singing. They're here. But let's have a drink together. He pulled from a pocket in his BC a half-pint bottle of bourbon.

That's pretty cool, said the boy, grinning.

You're sixteen now, old enough to take a drink.

It won't be the first, the boy said.

I know that too. Now climb into the tube and radio *Jealous Lady* to come pick us up. If you can sit on the edge and put your feet down on the net and maybe balance yourself it might help to keep the equipment dry.

The boy climbed into the tube then turned and looked at the man. If you're diving again I should wait.

Just do as I say, the man answered.

Yessir, the boy replied. He sat on the inside edge of the tube rocking in rhythm with the swells. He opened the Pelican case and switched on the GPS, making sure it faced up towards the invisible satellites. Upon dropping them off, the captain had marked a way point with his own GPS. He knew their starting position but not their rate of drift. When the coordinates appeared on the LED the boy switched on the radio. Come in *Jealous Lady*, he said, this is *Truck Tube*. Come in.

In a moment there was an answer. This is Cap'n Red aboard *Jealous Lady*. We hear you okay, *Truck Tube*. We're feeling better now. We're sober and we've caught two nice dorado. Where are you? The boy told him the coordinates and the captain repeated them.

The man floated silently, gripping the tube. He pictured the big diesels kicking in, the bow swinging around. He saw Red punching in the way point, getting his heading and range, and steaming towards them from beyond the horizon. He opened the bottle and handed it up to the boy, who took a swallow and handed it back.

The man then took a swallow and replaced the cap. I got to tell you boy, I ain't coming back.

What do you mean? the boy asked. His answer had come too suddenly to hide the anxiety.

I mean that I'm all tore up inside. Those doctors cut out most of my guts, but they didn't get all the bad stuff. The disease is spread through my body. I don't plan on dying in some hospital bed. She knows what I'm doing, but I didn't tell her when. That's your job when you get home. She'll understand and she'll need you to be strong. And Red knows it. We've been friends forty years, maybe more. Red knows too. He handed the bottle up. The boy unscrewed the cap and swallowed, choking the liquor down, eyes blank, face streaming with sea spray.

He handed back the bottle. You keep it, the man said. Don't be sad. There's nothing to be sad about. Help me into that rig. I'm not feeling too good. The boy unclipped the full scuba tank and, leaning over, helped the man into it. When everything was ready the man held onto the raft and instructed the boy to shoot a flare in ten minutes. Then he was gone.

He sat straddling the tube, one leg dangling over the side, one foot rising and falling on the shifting net floor. Overhead were clouds bunched and reefed in against the setting sun. Did their colors belong to the sea and sky, or could anyone claim them? Would he dream of mermaids?

After ten minutes he fired the flare gun, but there had been no need. From the southeast came *Jealous Lady* throwing spray, her diesels humming softly.

BLUE UNICORN

HIS FACE WAS A MUDSLIDE, STEEL-WOOL HAIR SUDSED WHITE in the sea mist. *But the Lord provided a great fish to swallow Jonah, and Jonah was inside the fish three days and three nights,* I quoted and heard the echo.

He looked my way, I thought, but the light and he were both dark. *And the Lord commanded the fish, and it vomited Jonah onto dry land,* I went on, flopping in the surf like a beached porpoise. Then I puked for the second or more probably the continuous time, watching neon pulses of discrete indigestibles flood the sparkling sand.

Her thoughts were a fish's: I held them, they were nothing. No great flight of alienness, just silence in place of the mewling noises that people make, jaws working silently up and down to pump water in, pump water out, sensuous lips more firm than cartilage and sucking around like bellows.

She's a fish, I announced. He didn't reply, believing me to be crazy or worse. However, I'm safe now, I continued. You can rest easy, I got well away.

Do you partake, my friend? I asked him. Are you a tonguer of Tabs, an imbiber of Blotter? Do you blow the Blue Unicorn, whisper Wedding Bells, sashay in the Sunshine, have a Ticket to ride? In short, do you deposit LSD into the closed system of yourself?

He looked my way casual as hell. No man, I'm a drunk.

Aha! Now we arrive at, as it were, the crux of the matter, the nexus, so to speak, the secret moist locus where something finally is sacred that's not surrounded by hair. A thing dark is right here among us lurking *and it is not nookie*, which in this desperate light resembles a small hummock in an unshaven swamp. Maybe sawgrass or cattails. Do you follow, fellow eremite?

I'm just your average drunk and we don't see much, even looking down at our feet.

I see *her*, or rather, I did.

Who, man?

Lucy in the Sky with Diamonds.

Them are stars, cousin, it's night. I see his head crank back like the pan of a tripod. I picture his eyes as dual telescopes dialing in the planets, dropping tears on their moons.

Moon their eyes, I say. I see her, I say. She's getting pumped by Bart Simpson plain as day, Lucy is, plain as your face, which isn't exactly because of the flowing of collagen downhill following that erosion map, the sharp inversion of the nose (nostrils pointed straight up), the eyebrows in a plate tectonic shift. Lookie there, behind us! See the brightness!

That ain't the sky, it's the casinos over Biloxi way lit up like Christmas. Folks are bleeding money, they sure are. He tipped back his head again and this time poured whiskey into an opening that was above the horizon but still invisible. The opening made smacking sounds, could be wet.

My God! She looked like a woman, but she was not a woman, my Lord no, she was a fish, some sort of bass, I think, or maybe a perch, a perciform fish. Her eyes were a permanent stare situation, irises like a fixed residency.

I'm requesting a neural transplant, I continued in a voice full of thoughts doubtfully obtuse. Sever the ganglia and substitute chips of silicon. (I waved my arms as a circuits check.) Extract the few brain cells left alive, detox in Thorazine, and grow on top of chips in a petri dish. Implant chips in skull, insert bone lid like manhole cover and suture flaps of skin, fire neurons. If I shit instead of uttering vowels, some random adjustment directed by control knobs sticking out of my head should do the trick. The docs and techs ought to have lots of laughs. Hey Harriett, want to see him piss and roll his eyes? Give that knob—yeah, that one—a quarter-turn to the left, yeah, that's right, good. Not too far or he'll anally crepitate all over your designer lab coat.

My premorbid adjustments are paltry notwithstanding, accounting for the recent bad trip. The soul is light and spongy as a crêpe, to which aforementioned bumpy ride attests. I can lie down on mine and roll up in it like it's a dirty blanket. Want to see? Watch.

Say, fool, don't be rolling around in that wet sand. I catch your drift. Bad acid trip. Flashbacks.

Flashbacks my ass! These visions are real. I *know* my mermaid, son, how she was conceived outside the body in cold seawater in an unlit drifting womb of mud and plankton. She wanted my sperm discharged around her in a cloud, she sought to wallow in sperm. External fertilization is all the rage out there down under, eggs and sperm everywhere, in your mouth, ears, gills. When we held hands her palm was slippery with ctenoid scales. Trust me, those Sirens don't sing to anyone unless they're another species semi-aquatic enough to climb out onto the rocks and reefs. Prufrock heard only the ringing of his ears. Ask yourself whether God stops breezes or brakes wind.

Now I can wonder, art thou a leg man? Interesting how a woman only five feet tall can't have truly great legs but one a mere six inches higher can dent hearts with hers, leave on a man's mind a lecherous image of the slinky form. Six inches make all the difference. I say the world turns on six inches, the length of my personal penis going unstated and unmeasured in present masculine company. Rest relaxed, I'm not one of *them*, no pecker waving from this collapsing window.

I'm a T and A man myself, he answers, Or used to be. I went in for a big set and wideness of butt. Nothing wasted, that's my motto. Got me in a dash of trouble too, heh, heh. He takes a swallow from the bottle, still standing.

You coming out of it, cousin? he asks. You were rolling around in the low surf sucking on a big dead fish when I first came on you. Someone had caught him way out in the Gulf and cut off the filets, and the remains washed ashore here on this beach. What you snuggled up beside of was a Sylvester-the-Cat kind of a fish, all head and a backbone and ribs, no meat left. Man, your mouth was pressed against those wet lips and giving them full tongue and your thumb was stuck in a hole where the heart must have been at one time, when that fish was alive and swimming on its way somewheres, and you were muttering on about what an icy bitch she was, and I asked who, and you said this goddamn mermaid without a beating heart.

Sleep's impossible. I have insomnia. Give me a drink.

I'm just an old sot, and I need this. I ain't got any money. You got money for another bottle?

Sure, but it's wet. Here. I reached into my pocket and handed over a wad of dripping bills. Keep it all. Buy us a bottle of mao-tai, at the very least cheap bourbon, after we finish here. His eyes got bright and his mudslide lifted in defiance of gravity, him staggering with the bottle an open cudgel and wiping off its mouth with a dirty sleeve in deference to me, a man of obvious taste and a connoisseur of cryptarithms.

At dawn and dusk we rose out of the dank sticky ooze to feed on tiny fishes, anchovies probably. I couldn't bear the taste and mixed mine (still wriggling) with a little floating Sargassum weed. Horrible. I appreciate antipasto as much as the next guy, but I like it to be dead. She would look at me through the gloom with her own dead eyes, never smiling, distracted by what I mistook for lust and expressed by rubbing against large amberjacks that tilted sideways reflecting silver.

Oh, no loyalty here! My mermaid was a group-spawner devoid of attachments, her blood the temperature of the sea, torso slippery, tail forked and barely sexy. Titties, you ask? To tell the truth, I can scarcely remember them, like sucking on scaled sushi. Not hair as we know hair, but more akin to the barbels of a catfish, trailing and fleshy and sticking out at all angles waving in the eddies. Hydra woman incarnate, but without the guile. She never could have come ashore or the stuff would mat and collapse into a mucous blob. No perms at thirty fathoms.

Conversation? Unexperienced and unknown, certainly. She grunted on the rare occasion, similar to a drum mind you, a blackened redfish. And I was, like, supposed to *undertand* this. She only really grunted loud when she wanted some sperm. Even then I had to do it myself by hand because I didn't want those cold slimy fins touching it after the first few times.

Penetration was out, you realize, as with most fish species, and everybody gets their jollies by administering a good fuck to the whole ocean and hoping a member of the opposite sex is close enough to be appreciative. Yessir, in ocean fucking propinquity is everything, X marks the spot, but at least you can't miss it.

Here, he said, take your ownself a teensie sip.

Thank you, I accept. Ah! The sweet restfulness of the dipsomaniac. Shorten your stature beside me on the beach.

That son of a bitch is wet. Me, I'll stand.

Acid parachutes your mind down onto very small and peculiar details, namely, in this instance, elemental components of the tidal wrack. With booze it's the other way around and everyone tries to solve no less peculiar problems like world hunger and the AIDS epidemic and how to keep the Christian Coalition off the Internet. Spaken thusly, hand over the bottle again so I can broaden my view. I'm bored with addressing sand gnats in an oratory voice, but that's hours in the past, maybe days ago, who knows. Either I was barfed up onto this beach by a quite large Jonah-fish or the sand gnats were already in my mouth from kissing a decaying carcass and got barfed up instead. I saw them dragging their tiny wings through it, mine or someone else's, one of *her* relatives.

Are you from these parts?

Which parts? This can't be Amurrica 'cause we're talking English here.

Gulfport, Mississippi, cousin.

I felt a silent spell creep near enough to grip hard. Flashback retroflexion soon to be garrulous again, enough time gathered within. Thoughts tend to digress and refract outward as the swimming mind nears the surface. I could scent loblollies from the piney woods beyond, hear angels squawk. Mineola's face bobbing from deep black water portended no fishy scales, was without slime except for a thin layer of diatoms such as encrust dead eyelids.

I drank only Laphroaig malt whiskey in those days, wore a Rolex watch and deck shoes made of breast leather from a peafowl. Assuming the perverse foppery of yachters, we stepped aboard our Shearwater 46 (stocked thoughtfully beforehand by servants) for a week-long cruise out to blue water, memory cupboards full of marlin skies and waves worn white on indigo. There was never any doubt, the wealth stacked cleanly atop fried catfish and hushpuppy franchises all over the South. Cat-and-pup magnate, that was us, or rather, me.

Lardly Towers, the mate, greeted us with salutes and the tanned helping hand aboard, after which he hummed relentlessly in falsetto much to the annoyance of our grim Ahab, Cap'n Dip Thong, late of Ho Chi Minh City by way of Bakersfield and Shreveport. A merry crew made merrier by well-stocked larders of pharmaceuticals and alcoholic toxicants to which everyone had a key. (Guests and Crew, attention! The marijuana bong is lit continuously!)

Mineola, the Lord bless her, shucked sandals on the aft deck and sat pensively sucking her left big toe (the one in ten lacking nail polish), foot anchored by breast shadows, and uttering labroidental musings from around her lip corners. At such times it was best to not speak harshly; I slunk away and made the rounds. We were self-contained for extended periods: forecabin fully *en suite*, the forward heads fronted by our cosy saloon with hideaway chart table, shipshape storage for fireworks, engine box hinged with gas strut for easy access, the butterfly skylight and exquisite joinery . . . I could go on. Beware, all fishes!

Mineola had been named by her father after a town in New York State and cursed a lifetime, through no fault of hers, by strangers mispronouncing it Minneapolis, even Minnehaha. To call her either one was a piss-off best avoided.

I signalled to cast lines ashore. Lardly hopped to, unmuzzling the mizzen (or whatever one does; to tell the truth, I'm not really a sailor), and we soon were astride the bounding main bucked this and that way by a devilish storm. We let baited handlines trail over the stern while Lardly stoked our mainsail, tweaked the jib, and Cap'n Dip Thong hove into such a wild reach that the sea thundered in fractured cataracts across the decks. Buoyed by immoderate quantities of Mind Detergent dampened with alcohol, I rolled with my fighting chair as the waves changed colors, head tipped back in the blissful rain, stabbing my tongue at the sea-ends of lightning bolts as might any cosmic sword-swallower.

Mineola—adequate if not spectacular in longness of the leg—was leaning over the rail of the pitching deck huffing greatly as she pulled in a line, butt cleavage pointed optimistically at the tattooed back, biceps bulging with the strain, when suddenly she flipped overboard.

Min! I shouted, trying desperately to untab a can of beer. But the sea overcame both shouts and grief: no matter how many cans I opened, the first swallow had a salty taint. Only afterwards did I learn that the captain had mistakenly put us on a northeasterly course. Ten days later we discovered ourselves becalmed in the Sargasso Sea, sails flapping like the wings of a moribund gull, stores depleted. Under a sobering sun I announced Min's fate; my crew had not noticed her absence but voted to mourn nonetheless.

Interrupted reverie. Did you come across any golden cities? he asks.

Golden cities? Mind moths unaccompanied by the dry heaves broke free and fluttered aimlessly.

Under the sea. With that mermaid bitch.

Ah, you mean cities of merfolk. The mythical cities of coral and pearl where a tail-flip sends you drifting along shaded avenues lined with giant kelp and the view through every-one's picture window is an aquarium scene. Sidewalks paved with gold and silver bullion from ancient shipwrecks, no hot-dog stands, just seafood wherever you turn. King Neptune runs a clam stand there.

I reckon so, yeah. I read somewheres that mermaids live in cities at the bottom of the sea. Is it true?

Naw, the closest thing I saw was an oyster-shell bank in Mobile Bay. Very dingy, more like a tenement. The place hadn't ever been dusted, and when you kicked your feet the shit-brown silt came billowing up at your face. The view also truly sucked.

So you don't believe in them?

I didn't say that. I only said that I never actually saw one. Maybe my little mermaid tootsie was an amberjack groupie, a seagoing Deadhead. Maybe her kick was following mi-grating fishes around hoping one might notice her and divulge a sperm cloud.

Hey, I don't need all this bread. Take it back except for a couple of twenties. I'm headed over to that Junior Food Mart across Route Whatsit back there for a sixer of cold Buds and maybe cigarettes and snacks. Men got to eat. You stay here and get warm. Sun coming up. Get us a bottle of good sip-ping whiskey too, but have to look around for that.

He recaptured both his mudslide and his hair and left.

I lay back in the wet sand. What I needed was a handful of morning glory seeds washed down with single-malt Scotch, maybe accompanied by a thai-stick. Somewhere palm fronds crackled and a gambler aboard a riverboat stuck squatly in the Mississippi mud gunned down his atavistic companion, who had insisted loudly that if riverboats can't float they at least ought to try. The assailant wore a sweatshirt that said Motherfucker, but there could have been two words or one hyphenated. I considered this effect to be merely hallucina-tory, not containing baroque overtones of any consequence, and searched my pockets for a bottle of dry Valium.

Creatures similar to angels or bats were in the air, disguised as crows. I noticed finally and accepted my personal layer

of encrusted diatoms as evidence of prolonged immer-
sion, exhuming memories of the glinting tapeta, the sprightly
filets . . . were you really? Her?

ABOUT THE AUTHOR

STEPHEN SPOTTE, a marine scientist at the University of Connecticut, was born and raised in West Virginia. He holds a bachelor's degree from Marshall University and a doctorate from the University of Southern Mississippi. He is author of eighty scientific articles and eight nonfiction books. An earlier collection of his short fiction, *An Optimist in Hell*, is also available from Creative Arts Books.